THE
LONELY GHOST

Mike Ford

THE
LONELY GHOST

Mike Ford

Scholastic Inc.

Copyright © 2022 by Mike Ford

All rights reserved. Published by Scholastic Inc., *Publishers since 1920*. SCHOLASTIC and associated logos are trademarks and/or registered trademarks of Scholastic Inc.

The publisher does not have any control over and does not assume any responsibility for author or third-party websites or their content.

No part of this publication may be reproduced, stored in a retrieval system, or transmitted in any form or by any means, electronic, mechanical, photocopying, recording, or otherwise, without written permission of the publisher. For information regarding permission, write to Scholastic Inc., Attention: Permissions Department, 557 Broadway, New York, NY 10012.

This book is a work of fiction. Names, characters, places, and incidents are either the product of the author's imagination or are used fictitiously, and any resemblance to actual persons, living or dead, business establishments, events, or locales is entirely coincidental.

ISBN 978-1-338-75797-2

10 9 8 7 6 5 4 3 2   22 23 24 25 26

Printed in the U.S.A.   40

First edition, June 2022

Book design by Stephanie Yang

For Eva Galli

1

"Ouch!"

Ava peered at her fingertip, where a bead of blood was forming. She stuck her finger in her mouth and glared at the rosebush she had been hacking away at with a pair of clippers. Her blood tasted coppery on her tongue and made her feel sick. She took her finger out and pressed her thumb against the spot where the thorn had pricked her. There was a little sliver of black visible beneath the pale pink skin.

"You need to get that out," Cassie said. "You could get sporotrichosis."

"Sporowhat?" Ava asked.

Her sister swept her long, dark hair out of her face and tucked it behind her ear. She, of course, was wearing gloves. "An infection caused by *Sporothrix schenckii*," she said. "It's a fungus that grows on rose thorns, among other places," she added when Ava stared at her with one eyebrow cocked. "Named after Benjamin Schenck, the medical student who first discovered it, in 1896."

"Oh, right," Ava said. "Benjamin Schenck." She pointed at Cassie with the clippers. "Why do you know these things?"

"I was reading up about roses," Cassie said. "Because of the garden and the Blackthorn roses. It just came up."

"Most girls our age read about pop stars," Ava teased.

"Most girls our age are boring," said Cassie. "Now, go wash your hands and use tweezers to get the splinter out. Don't forget to put some ointment on it. Just in case."

"Just in case," Ava repeated as she turned and walked toward the house. "Got it."

"You'll be sorry when your hand falls off and you can't be a catcher anymore!" Cassie called after her.

"Goalie!" Ava called back, laughing.

Sometimes, she couldn't believe she and Cassie were twins. She had short blonde hair cut in a modern style. Cassie, with her long curls, looked like something out of an old-fashioned photograph. Where Cassie loved reading books and playing video games alone, Ava was all about soccer and hanging out with her friends. In many ways, they were total opposites. But they also got along really well. Usually.

This was a particularly good thing at the moment, because their parents had uprooted them from their home in the city and moved them to the little town of Ebenezer two weeks ago. Right now they were the only friends each other had. At least until school started in a few days. Ava was excited about that. Cassie was less thrilled. But it would be fine. It always was. Ava would make new friends easily, and she would make sure her sister was included in things, the way she always did.

She clomped up the wide stairs to the front porch, pushed open the door, and went into the house. She still wasn't used to living there, and to her it felt like they were staying at a hotel. A very old, very big, very run-down hotel. *You need to start thinking of it as home*, she told herself as she went into the kitchen.

"How are things going in the garden?" her mother asked, unwrapping newspaper from around a glass she'd taken out of the cardboard moving box on the counter and setting the glass in a cabinet.

"It's fighting back," Ava said as she turned on the water in the sink. There was a loud rumbling, followed by what sounded like a belch, and the faucet spat out a glob of brownish water. Ava let the water run for a minute, until it was clear. Then she soaped up her hands and rinsed them.

"I know you girls have been working hard on it for a couple of days, but it still looks like a forest out there," Ava's mother said. "You haven't even gotten close to the summerhouse."

The summerhouse was what her mother called the small building in the center of the garden. It did resemble a house—actually a much smaller version of the big one. It was called the summerhouse because in the days before the big house had air-conditioning, people would sit or sometimes sleep in there when the weather was hot.

"Good thing summer is pretty much over, then," Ava said. She picked up the knife that her mother was using to cut the tape on the moving boxes and started poking at the splinter in her finger.

"It's still a feature," her mother said. "We can decorate it for holidays, and when there are weddings here, guests can take pictures in it."

"Once Dad rebuilds it, that is," said Ava. "What's that, item number 3,798 on his list?"

"It will all get done," her mother said. She sighed. "I hope."

Buying Blackthorn House had mostly been Ava's father's idea. Tired of the long hours he spent at his job as an accountant for a carpet store, he'd decided he—meaning all of them—needed to make a big change. He'd found Blackthorn House on a website that featured old houses for sale and decided it would make the perfect bed-and-breakfast. So now they were fixing up the run-down place and starting their new lives as innkeepers.

"I promise we'll be open by Christmas!" Ava's father announced, walking into the kitchen. He waved a pad of paper at them. "In fact, I just booked the first rooms."

"You're taking reservations?" Ava's mother said.

"Who would book this place with it looking the way it does?" Ava asked. Her finger was bleeding again from all the prodding with the knife, but at least she had gotten the splinter out. She washed it down the drain and rinsed her finger again.

"A couple who remembers what it looked like when the rose garden was still beautiful," her father said. "They heard the house had been bought and that it was being restored to its original glory."

Ava had seen photographs of the Blackthorn House garden. It *had* been spectacular. She had serious doubts that they would ever be able to get it looking like that again. The rosebushes hadn't been attended to since the death of the house's last owner, Lily Blackthorn, nearly twenty years ago. Even before that, Lily had let them become overgrown and wild. They had completely surrounded the summerhouse and looked like they were trying to strangle it. Every time she went out there, Ava pictured the castle where Sleeping Beauty lay enchanted, waiting for Prince Phillip to cut through the forest of thorns and wake her up. "He'd need a flamethrower to get through this one," Ava had joked to Cassie.

She opened one of the drawers to look for the ointment and a bandage. Lying on top of the assorted odds and ends that had already accumulated there since their arrival was a sheet of paper. Ava picked it up. "Dad," she said, realizing what it was. "Did you forget to mail in my application for the soccer team?"

"No," her father said. "I put it in the envelope that was on the counter and . . ." He looked at the application that Ava was waving in his face. "And I think I must have mailed the school my application for a business license instead. Sorry, honey."

"Dad, the application deadline was yesterday," Ava said.

"Let's drive over to the school right now," her father suggested. "We'll take your application. I'm sure one day won't matter. I mean, how many kids are going to sign up for soccer in a town this size?"

The woman behind the counter in the Patience Prufrock Central School office shook her head. "I'm sorry," she said, "but there's nothing I can do. The team is full. Soccer is our most popular activity."

"What about alternates?" Ava asked.

"Full," the woman said firmly. "But we have a number of other activities you can sign up for."

"I want to play soccer," Ava said glumly as the woman opened a folder of sign-up sheets and riffled through them.

"Here's a good one," the woman said, taking out a sheet. "Drama Club. That would be oh-so-much fun."

Ava groaned.

"What did you say your last name was?" the woman asked, ignoring her obvious lack of interest.

"Chapel," Ava said. "Ava Chapel."

"Are you related to a Cassandra Chapel?"

"Cassie," said Ava. "She's my sister. We're twins."

"Well, your sister is already signed up for Drama Club," the woman informed her. "You'd be in it together."

Ava turned to her father. "You mailed Cassie's form in, but not mine?"

Her father shook his head. "She never gave me one. She must have mailed it in herself."

The woman behind the desk was looking at Ava expectantly. "So, shall I put you down?" she asked. "It's that, the debate team, or Fudge Club."

"Fudge Club?"

"Baking," the woman explained.

"How about I don't do any activity?" Ava said to her father.

"You have to have one," the woman said. "It's a school requirement."

Ava glared at her father, who looked sheepish. "Fine," she said. "Sign me up for Drama."

When she got home, she found Cassie in the third-floor bedroom she had claimed for her own. "When did you sign up for Drama Club?" Ava asked.

Cassie, who was busy removing old gold-and-green-striped paper from one of the walls, said, "Last week. I saw the deadline was coming up, and I wasn't about to trust Dad to do it. You know how distracted he's been. Why?"

Ava threw herself down on Cassie's bed and groaned. "Because I *did* trust him, and he didn't do it. Now I have to do Drama Club."

Cassie laughed. "Well, you should be great at it," she said. "You're being *very* dramatic right now."

"Ha-ha," said Ava. "How would you feel if you'd missed out on Drama and had to play soccer?"

Cassie made a horrified snorting sound.

"Exactly," Ava said.

"Maybe somebody on the team will quit," Cassie suggested. "Or get hurt."

It wasn't the nicest thought, but it was exactly what Ava had been secretly thinking. Sometimes, the twin thing expressed itself in surprising ways.

"Anyway, come look at what I found," Cassie said.

Ava sat up. Cassie had moved to a part of the wall where the paper was almost completely gone except for a few stubborn patches here and there. Ava went over to where she was standing. The wall beneath the paper had originally been painted a light blue color, which was now faded and stained. Cassie was pointing to what looked like a child's drawing, a hastily scribbled stick figure with straw-like hair sticking out of a head that had two black dots for eyes and a larger circle for a mouth. The figure was clothed in a crudely drawn dress, and underneath it the name "Rosemary" was written in crooked capital letters.

"I wonder who drew that?" Ava said.

"It looks like a kid did it," said Cassie.

"That's probably why they put up wallpaper," said Ava. She looked at the figure more closely. "She looks like she's screaming. It's creepy."

"I think it's interesting," Cassie said. "It's part of the house's past."

"Until you paint over it," said Ava, returning to the bed. "Did you pick a color yet?"

"I'm thinking purple," Cassie said.

So much for the twin thing, Ava thought. She hated

purple. But what she said was "That will be pretty."

Cassie pulled another strip of paper off the wall. "What do you think the people who lived here before us were like?"

"I don't know," said Ava. "I mean, the woman who owned it was like three thousand years old, right?"

"Probably not quite *that* old," Cassie said. "I wonder if she had any kids, or grandkids. Maybe even great-grandkids."

"If she did, why didn't they want the house?" Ava asked. "Nobody has lived here in years. It's kind of weird when you think about it. Why was one old lady in this huge house all by herself? And why did nobody want to live here?"

"Maybe it's been waiting for the right people," Cassie suggested. "Us."

"Great," said Ava. "Now the house has feelings? What happens if it *doesn't* like us?"

Cassie ignored her and ran her fingertips over the wall.

"Maybe Rosemary was one of her kids," she said. "Maybe this used to be her room."

Ava looked at the drawing of the girl on the wall. She had thought it was creepy before. Now it was even creepier. She would be glad when Cassie painted over it. *Even if it is purple,* she thought.

2

"Here goes nothing," Ava said as the school bus came to a stop in front of the house and the doors slid open.

She stepped on first. Cassie followed her. Ava quickly scanned the bus to see what seats were available, then headed to an empty one halfway down the aisle, in what she always thought of as the Neutral Zone. The back of a bus was where the older or more popular kids sat. The front was for the youngest ones and the ones who needed to get homework done before they got to school. It was usually better to be farther back, but since it was their first day, they had to make do with what was open.

She knew all eyes were on them, but she didn't let that bother her. She actually kind of liked it. They were the new girls in school. Everybody would wonder about them, and nobody would know anything. It was a chance for them to be whoever they wanted to be. She waited for Cassie to slide into the spot by the window, then sat down next to her. Cassie opened her backpack, took out a book, and started to read.

Ava scoped out the other kids as much as she was able to. She didn't dare turn around to see who was seated in the back, as that would be too obvious. She had to content herself with observing who was visible from her seat. That was mostly younger kids, and they weren't very interesting. She sighed and settled in for the ride.

"Hey," a girl's voice said from immediately behind her. "Is that an Isobel Bird novel?"

It took a moment for Ava to realize that the person was speaking to Cassie and not to her. Cassie, engrossed in the book, didn't even notice. Ava nudged her with an elbow.

"What?" Cassie yelped.

"I asked if that was an Isobel Bird novel," the voice said again.

Ava turned her head, sneaking a quick look at the girl. She was Black, and her hair was done up in beautiful Dutch braids that made Ava momentarily jealous that she had cut all her hair off over the summer. She also noticed a pair of soccer cleats sitting on the seat beside the girl.

"Yeah," Cassie said. *"In the Dreaming.* It's—"

"Number five in the series," the girl said. "I know. My favorite is number eleven, *The House of Winter.* I'm Gwen."

"Cassie," Cassie said. "And this is Ava."

"Hey," Gwen said to Ava.

"You play soccer?" Ava asked.

Gwen nodded. "Striker," she said. "You two play?"

"I do," Ava said. "Goalie. But I didn't sign up in time."

The bus stopped, the doors opened, and a girl got on. Olive-skinned, with short dark hair and a thin build, she carried her stuff in what looked like a yellow teddy bear that had had the stuffing pulled out of it. She made a bee-line for Gwen's seat, plopping down next to her.

"This is Aisha," Gwen announced. Then she said to Aisha, "This is Ava and Cassie. They're the ones who moved into Blackthorn House."

"Really?" Aisha said. She looked at Gwen sideways. "Did you tell them about the ghost?"

Gwen smacked her in the arm, but not hard. "No, I did not. You don't meet people for the first time and five minutes later say, 'So, did you know you live in a haunted house?'"

"Haunted house?" Ava said.

"It's not haunted," Aisha said quickly.

"Too late," said Gwen. "You already mentioned it. Now you have to tell them the whole story."

Aisha looked like she wished she had never said anything. "It's not that big a deal," she said. "There are just some people who think your house is haunted, is all."

"Some people?" Gwen said. "More like everybody in town."

"Not everybody," Aisha said.

"Everybody," Gwen repeated, as if this were the last word on the subject.

"What's this about a ghost?" Ava pressed.

"There's a ghost that walks around," Gwen said after Aisha just shook her head and didn't answer. "Some people have seen her in the windows. Others have seen her in the garden. Bobby Endicott went in there on a dare once and he said the ghost came down the stairs holding her own head."

"Bobby Endicott also claimed that aliens abducted him and took out his appendix," Aisha said. "Anyway, I don't believe in ghosts."

"You don't have to believe in them for them to be real," said Gwen.

"Have either of you seen this ghost?" Ava asked them.

Aisha shook her head again. Ava waited for Gwen to say that she had absolutely seen the ghost for herself. After a pause, though, she shook her head too. "I just heard about it," she admitted. "Have you seen anything weird there since you moved in?"

Ava thought about the drawing on Cassie's wall. She waited to see if Cassie would mention it. But her sister wasn't saying anything at all. "Nothing," Ava said.

"Cassie's reading an Isobel Bird book," Gwen told Aisha, as if the ghost was old news now. "Number five."

"Cool!" Aisha exclaimed. "I like number three best." She looked at Ava. "What's your favorite?"

"Oh, um, I haven't read them," Ava said.

"You *need* to," Aisha said. Her face lit up. "We should start a book club," she said. "We can all read the same book and then have a sleepover and talk about it. But nothing any of us have already read. Something new."

Ava was surprised to see Cassie turn to the girls and say, "That sounds fun."

Gwen shrugged. "Sure," she said.

"How about you, Ava?" Aisha asked. "Are you in?"

Ava wasn't sure how to respond. From the sound of it, the girls were into fantasy books, which weren't really her thing. But it was unusual for Cassie to show interest in making new friends, and she herself liked the idea of having other girls to do stuff with, so she said, "Totally in."

"Great," Aisha said. "I'll look up some books in the library and we can decide on one at lunch, okay?"

"That reminds me," Gwen said, unzipping her backpack and rooting around in it. "What classes do we have together?"

Aisha opened her bear bag and took out a piece of paper. Cassie did the same, unfolding it and handing it to Gwen.

"Where's yours?" Gwen asked Ava.

"Oh, Cassie and I have the same schedule," Ava explained. "They always do that, because we're twins and they think we have to do everything together."

"Twins?" Gwen said. She looked from one to the other.

Here it comes, Ava thought. *She's going to say we don't look anything alike.*

"Which one's older?" Gwen asked, surprising her.

"I am," Ava said. "By seven minutes."

"And when's your birthday?"

"August seventeenth," said Ava.

"Mine's June thirtieth," Gwen said. "Aisha's isn't until October. That makes me the oldest."

"She means she thinks she's the boss," Aisha said, rolling her eyes.

Gwen ignored her and looked at their schedules. "We have a bunch of classes together," she said. "And the three of you are in Drama Club."

"I can't wait to find out what show we're doing this year," Aisha said. "Mr. Chowdry and Mrs. Randall always pick something really fun."

"Mr. Chowdry is the English teacher," Gwen told them. "Mrs. Randall teaches music. Do you two sing?"

"I don't," Ava said. "But Cassie does. Really well."

"Only when I'm in my bedroom," Cassie said, blushing.

"I can't sing either," Gwen said. "Aisha's pretty good,

though. Last year we did *The Sound of Music* and she was one of the kids."

"Brigitta," Aisha said.

"She had a solo," Gwen said.

"It was one line," said Aisha, standing up.

Ava had been so focused on the conversation with their new friends that she hadn't even realized they'd reached the school. Now the bus doors opened. Everybody filed off and headed inside.

"Seventh grade is this way," Gwen told them as they walked down a hallway. "Homerooms are assigned alphabetically by last name. You're Chapels. I saw it on your paper. Aisha's name is Bashir, so you all will be together. I'm a Wright, so I'll be in another room. But I'll see you first period for science."

Aisha stopped at one of the doors. Gwen waved and kept going. The three girls entered their classroom, where a woman stood next to a desk, looking at a piece of paper.

"That's Ms. Gonnick," Aisha said as they found three empty desks in a row and sat down. "She teaches math."

A loud bang ricocheted through the room as the door slammed against the wall, making everyone turn around to look. In the doorway stood a tall girl with blonde hair pulled into a single long braid, and tanned skin that made her look as if she'd spent the whole summer lying on a beach.

"Ugh," Aisha groaned. "Beth-Ann Jennings. I'd hoped since she's a *J* that she would be in the next homeroom."

Beth-Ann smiled as if she were posing for a photograph. "Sorry about the big bang," she said. "I didn't mean to hit the door so hard."

"She's not sorry one bit," Aisha said as Beth-Ann strolled into the room.

The girl walked past them, then stopped and turned around. "You're new," she said.

"No, I've been here since first grade," Aisha said. "You just never noticed."

Beth-Ann's smile tightened. "Not *you*," she said. "Them."

"I'm Ava, and this is my sister, Cassie," Ava said.

Beth-Ann looked Cassie up and down. "Can't you talk?" she asked.

Ava started to respond, but bit her lip. Cassie was going to have to handle this on her own. She could sense how tense her sister was. She reached over beneath the desks and took her hand, squeezing it.

"I can talk just fine," Cassie said, as if Ava's fingers were pressing a button that allowed her mouth to work. "When there's someone I want to talk to."

Beth-Ann's smile tightened even more, like someone had wound a key at the back of her head a little too far. She walked away, taking a seat next to a girl with red hair. She said something to the girl, who turned and looked at Cassie and Ava. Then she and Beth-Ann laughed loudly.

"Well, I'm off to a great start," Cassie said.

"Don't worry about it," Aisha told her. "Beth-Ann would

have found some reason to dislike you sooner or later anyway. At least you got it over with fast."

"What's her problem?" Ava asked.

"Her uncle is a TV director out in Hollywood," Aisha said. "She got to be an extra on one of his shows once, so she thinks she's famous. Also, her mother is the mayor."

A bell sounded, and Ms. Gonnick stepped to the front of the room. "Welcome to the first day of seventh grade," she said. "Most of you were in this same school last year and know your way around, but I see we have two new students."

Everyone except Beth-Ann and the red-haired girl looked at Ava and Cassie.

"In order to help you get familiar with the school and your classmates, you've each been assigned a student ambassador for the day. Which one of you is Cassie?"

Cassie raised her hand.

Ms. Gonnick looked at the paper she was holding. "Cassie, your ambassador is Aisha Bashir."

Cassie looked relieved.

"Aisha can be the ambassador for both of us," Ava said. "Since we already know her."

"You must be Ava," Ms. Gonnick said. "Thank you for the suggestion, Ava, but I think we should stick with the plan. Which means that your ambassador is" she looked at the paper again—"Beth-Ann Jennings."

Ava felt her stomach sink. Beth-Ann turned around slowly, a smile plastered to her face, but it was about as fake as a plastic plant. Ava knew the girl didn't want to show her around any more than Ava wanted her to. But she flashed a fake smile right back at Beth-Ann.

It was going to be a long day.

3

"I'm supposed to eat lunch with you and introduce you to my friends," Beth-Ann said as she and Ava walked toward the cafeteria after fourth period. "You can sit with us, but don't talk unless someone asks you a question. And don't think it means anything. We're just being nice."

"Thanks," Ava said, "but I'll sit with my sister and *our* friends."

"That's not how this whole ambassador thing works," said Beth-Ann. "I get extra credit for this, so you're going to do what—"

"I'll see you for English next period," Ava said,

interrupting her. She pushed open the door to the lunch-room and paused, searching the tables for Cassie and the others. When she found them, she walked over and pulled out a chair, sitting down with a huge sigh.

"Are you and Beth-Ann BFFs yet?" Gwen asked.

Ava opened her backpack and took out the bag lunch she'd packed that morning. "Totally," she said. "In fact, I asked her to join our book group and she said sure. The first sleepover is at her house."

The other three stared at her, their mouths open. Ava let them wait while she unwrapped her ham-and-cheese sand-wich, took a big bite, and swallowed.

"I'm kidding," she said. "I'd rather eat bugs."

The girls exhaled. "Don't scare us like that," Aisha said. She opened her bear backpack and took something out. "But speaking of our club, I think I found our first book."

Ava looked at the cover of the book Aisha was holding up. The picture on it showed a girl in front of a mirror with an ornate gold frame. Reflected in the mirror was the face of someone who looked a lot like the girl, but dressed in clothes from an earlier era. That girl had a terrified look on her face. An ominous figure loomed behind her, and a hand reached out over her shoulder, the fingertips protruding through the glass of the mirror. The title of the book was *Sisters in Time*, and it was by an author named Taraji Lang.

"Has anyone read it? Aisha asked.

All the girls shook their heads.

"Good," said Aisha. "Mr. Monday says he can get three more copies from interlibrary loan. Or you can read it electronically if that's your thing."

"What's it about?" Ava asked. The cover made her think it was probably something scary, and although she wasn't afraid of too many things, horror wasn't her favorite genre.

"It's a ghost story," Aisha said, confirming her suspicions. "I guess I had ghosts on my mind because of, you know, what we talked about on the bus this morning. We can read something else if you don't like this one."

"It sounds great," Ava said quickly. She could tell that

Aisha and Gwen were already sold on the book, and she knew Cassie would be into the story. She also knew that if Cassie thought *Ava* didn't want to read the book, she would pretend that she didn't want to either. It was the twin thing again.

"Okay!" Aisha said. "When should we have our sleepover, and where?"

"How about this Saturday?" Gwen suggested.

"That's fine for me," said Aisha. "We shouldn't have much homework this first week, and that gives us time to read. But we can't do it at my house. My father is having a cookout to celebrate his bowling team winning first place in their league, and there will be way too many people around."

"My brother's band practices at our house on Saturdays," Gwen said. "You don't want to be around for that."

"Are they that bad?" Ava asked.

"No, they're really good," said Gwen. "But they're loud. We wouldn't be able to hear ourselves talk. My parents and

I usually go out to dinner and a movie when they're there."

"We could do it at our house," Cassie said.

Ava was surprised to hear her make that suggestion. "Our place is a mess," she reminded her. "We're in the middle of renovations," she explained to Gwen and Aisha.

"The kitchen works," said Cassie. "So do the bathrooms. And we have enough beds."

"I'm sure it'll be fine," Gwen said. "Besides, I'd love to see the inside of Blackthorn House."

Ava couldn't think of any other argument for not doing it. "We'll have to ask Mom," she said. But she knew her mother would say okay.

"This will be so much fun," Aisha said, as if the matter was settled.

As Cassie and the other two continued to talk about the book, Ava ate her lunch. It wasn't that she didn't want the girls to come over, or to read the book, so she wasn't sure why she was feeling hesitant about the whole thing. She glanced over at the table where Beth-Ann sat with a handful of other girls. As if sensing that she was being watched, Beth-Ann looked up, and for a moment their eyes met. Beth-Ann frowned and looked away.

I don't know where I fit in, Ava thought.

She didn't know why this idea had popped into her head, but it was sort of true. She definitely didn't belong with Beth-Ann or anyone who would hang around her. And although she really liked Aisha and Gwen, they seemed to have more in common with Cassie than with her. She wasn't used to that. Usually, it was the other way around.

Ava really wished she had gotten onto the soccer team. There, she would definitely have met other girls like herself. She envied Gwen that she was getting to play. There was nothing that she could do about it, though. *Maybe Drama Club will be fun*, she told herself.

After lunch, she reteamed with Beth-Ann, who basically ignored her when they were walking alone together and pretended to be helpful when they were in classes. By the time the last bell rang, Ava was more than ready to go home. When she stepped on the bus, she was surprised to see Cassie and Aisha already sitting together. She took the empty seat in front of them.

"Gwen has soccer practice," Aisha said.

"Lucky her," Ava muttered.

"The first Drama Club meeting is tomorrow," Aisha continued, not noticing Ava's bad mood. "I can't wait to find out what show we're doing."

"Do you have a favorite?" Cassie asked her.

Aisha laughed. "All of them," she said. "I've been practicing songs from some of the most popular ones, so I'm prepared for anything."

Cassie and Aisha continued to talk about the show the whole way home. When the bus reached Blackthorn House, the twins said goodbye to Aisha and got off.

"I really like Aisha and Gwen," Cassie said as they walked up the path to the porch. "I'm sorry you had to spend so much time with Beth-Ann."

"Me too," Ava said. "At least it was just for today. Tomorrow will be better."

When they went into the house, they were greeted by the sight of their father standing in the front parlor, covered in white dust. He was holding a sledgehammer, and a good part of the plaster that covered the walls was in a huge pile around his feet. Seeing the girls, he lowered the mask that covered his mouth and nose, revealing a circular area of clean face.

"Hey," he said. "How was the first day?"

"Great," Cassie said, while Ava remained silent. "What are you doing?"

"We need to update the electrical wiring," her father answered. "That means all of this plaster has to go."

"It looks like a snow globe in here," Cassie remarked.

Ava was looking into the hole their father had made in the wall. "There's newspaper stuffed in here," she said, reaching in and pulling out a wadded-up ball.

"They used to put all kinds of things in the walls to

insulate them," her father said. "And that's not all that's in there. I found some other stuff too. It's in that box." He pointed to a cardboard box sitting on the floor near the fireplace.

Ava went over and looked in the box. Inside were half a dozen items, including a large glass marble, a toy wooden horse, an unopened packet of Boy-O-Boy marigold seeds, a pencil with COOLEY'S TRACTOR & FEED stamped on the side in gold, a faded photograph of two girls in old-fashioned striped swimsuits standing on a beach with their arms around each other's waists, and a rectangular plastic thing that Ava couldn't identify. "What's this?" she asked, holding it up.

Her father laughed. "I guess you're too young to have ever seen one of those," he said. "It's a cassette tape. It's what we had before CDs and iTunes and Spotify. We used to record music on them."

"How'd all this stuff get inside the wall?" Cassie said. She was holding the photograph of the two girls in her hand and examining it.

"Things end up in walls all the time," their father said. "They fall down vents, or through cracks. Sometimes people hide things on purpose and forget."

Cassie was looking at the back of the picture. "This has 'Lily and Violet, 1915, age 10' written on it," she said. "Wasn't the woman who lived here named Lily Blackthorn?"

"Yep," her father confirmed.

"Did she have a sister?" Cassie asked.

"I have no idea, honey," their father said. "I don't really know anything about her except that she was the last person in her family, which is why nobody inherited the house after she died."

Ava was examining the cassette tape. There was a label on one side, and something was written on it. But the handwriting was hard to read, and the ink had been smeared at some point. "Do you think we can still play this?" she asked.

"Unless it somehow got erased, sure," her father said. "We just need a cassette player."

"Do we have one?"

Her father scratched his beard, creating a cloud of plaster dust. "I think there might still be a boom box in one of the boxes in the garage."

"Boom box?" said Cassie.

"Another piece of ancient technology," their father said. "I'll look for it in a little bit, okay?"

Ava and Cassie went upstairs to their rooms. After Ava dropped her bag in her room, she went down the hall to Cassie's. Her sister was sitting on the bed, looking at the photo of Violet and Lily Blackthorn, which she had brought up with her. Ava sat down next to her. Her eyes instinctively went to the drawing of the girl on the wall. "Doesn't it creep you out, having that there?" she said.

"What?" said Cassie. She followed Ava's gaze. "Rosemary? No. I kind of like her. Hey, look at this picture. Do you think Lily and Violet were twins?"

Ava took the photo and looked at it more closely than she had before. The girls were the same height, with the same dark hair and round faces. They weren't identical, though. Their features were different. Also, one was smiling happily, while the other looked almost sad.

"It says 'age 10' on the back," Cassie said. "So they must be the same age, or it would have two numbers."

"They could be related some other way," Ava suggested. "Like cousins. Or they could just be friends." She handed the photo back.

Cassie continued to stare at the image of the two girls. "Blackthorn House is full of secrets," she said in a whisper.

"What?" said Ava.

Cassie looked at her. "I didn't say anything."

"Yes, you did," Ava insisted. "You said 'Blackthorn House is full of secrets.'"

"I must have been thinking it and didn't realize I wasn't using my inside voice," Cassie joked. She set the photo of the Blackthorn girls on top of the book on her bedside table. "We should probably go downstairs and help Dad clean up."

When they got downstairs, their father was plugging

something into an outlet in the kitchen. "I found the boom box," he said. "Let's see if it still works."

He pushed a button, and lights on the box came alive. He touched something else and a little door in the front popped open. He took the cassette tape and put it inside, then closed the compartment again. "Here we go," he said, pressing yet another button.

The sound of hissing filled the air. This went on for a few seconds, and Ava thought maybe there was nothing on the tape, or that it had been ruined somehow. Then a woman's voice spoke. "This is the night of Wednesday, September thirteenth, 1978," she said. "It is the anniversary of the death of Violet Blackthorn, and we are here to communicate with her spirit."

Ava felt a chill wrap around her. She looked at Cassie. "Is this what I think it is?" she said.

Cassie's eyes were wide. She nodded. When she spoke, her voice was a whisper. "They're holding a séance."

4

"Absolutely not."

"Why not?" Ava said.

Her mother, removing the cassette tape from the boom box, held it up. "Because," she said, "it will give you nightmares. Remember what happened when you watched that movie about the ghost hunters? You slept with the lights on for a month."

"That was different!" Ava objected. "You could *see* the ghosts. This is just people talking. Besides, it's, like, important historical research. Right, Cassie?"

She glanced over at her sister, expecting Cassie to back her up. But Cassie only shrugged.

"What?" Ava exclaimed. "Come on. You know you want to hear what's on there as much as I do."

"Maybe your mother is right," her father said before Cassie could answer.

Ava let out a groan of frustration. "What is *wrong* with all of you?" she said. "This is the most interesting thing we've found since we moved into this dump."

"It's not a dump," her mother said, sounding annoyed. "And that settles it. Now, go wash up for dinner."

Ava left the room. Cassie followed her, and together they went upstairs.

"Why didn't you back me up?" Ava asked.

"I don't know," Cassie admitted. "Part of me wanted to hear what's on the tape. But another part of me was scared."

"Of what?" Ava said. "You're the one who usually likes scary stuff. Not me."

"I know," Cassie agreed.

Ava waited for her to say more, but Cassie remained silent as they went into their shared bathroom on the second floor. Ava turned on the water. As she washed her hands, she looked at Cassie's expression in the mirror. Her twin had a strange look on her face, as if she were listening to something that Ava couldn't hear. Then Cassie nodded.

"What are you doing?" Ava asked.

"What?" Cassie said, shaking her head, as if Ava had awakened her from a nap.

"You looked like someone was talking to you," Ava said, handing Cassie the soap and rinsing her hands under the faucet. "It was kind of weird. Like you were in a daze or something."

"Well, I wasn't," Cassie said defensively.

Ava dried her hands on a towel. She didn't wait for Cassie to finish before she left the bathroom and went downstairs. She was still mad. She stayed mad all through dinner, barely answering when anyone asked her a question about her day, then all through doing dishes. If Cassie noticed that her sister was ignoring her as she passed her the soapy plates and silverware to rinse, she didn't let on, which only made Ava more annoyed. When the last dish was dried and put away, Ava stomped upstairs to her bedroom, shut the door, and flung herself down on her bed. She waited for Cassie to come knocking, as she usually did whenever they were having one of their rare disagreements, but half an hour went by without a rap on the door.

When an hour had passed, Ava realized that Cassie probably wasn't going to come to her. And she certainly wasn't going to go to Cassie's room. After all, Cassie was in the wrong. At least, that's how Ava felt about it. Her sister should have taken her side about listening to the tape. *Especially after I agreed to do the book group*, she thought angrily.

The first day of school certainly hadn't gone the way she'd hoped it would. She liked their new friends, but everything else was kind of awful. No soccer. Having to be in

Drama Club. Beth-Ann Jennings. It was about as different from the great day she'd pictured in her head as it could get. What she really needed right now was her twin to make her laugh and to tell her that everything would be different tomorrow. But Cassie wasn't there.

She took out her schoolbooks and distracted herself by doing the little bit of homework they'd been assigned. After that, she tried to go online, but the Wi-Fi kept going out. Eventually, she turned the computer off in frustration. With nothing else to do, she flopped onto the bed and picked up a soccer magazine. She was partway through an interview with Megan Rapinoe when the lights flickered. They did it several more times, rapidly going on and off, before going out and staying off.

This was not unusual. The house's ancient wiring often acted up, particularly if too many things were running at once. It generally came on again pretty quickly, though, so Ava waited in the darkness for that to happen. But a couple of minutes went by without the power coming back on.

That meant one or both of her parents were probably in the basement changing out a blown fuse.

Although she hated to admit it, Ava was afraid of the dark. She especially didn't like being *alone* in the dark. She didn't like not being able to see what was around her, not being able to tell if someone—or something—was sneaking up on her. Lying on her bed with the darkness all around her, Ava could all too easily imagine that every bump and groan the old house made was really the sound of something crawling down the hallway or sneaking a hand, tentacle, or claw out from beneath the bed to reach up and grab her foot.

She drew her legs up and held her breath, listening for the sound of her parents moving around downstairs. *The lights should have come on by now*, she thought. What was taking them so long? Her heart began to race as all kinds of unpleasant thoughts flooded her head. Thoughts that made her even more anxious about what might be lurking in the dark.

She heard a rustling sound, imagined what might have made it, and got up and ran to her door. Flinging it open, she walked quickly down the hallway, past the bathroom, to Cassie's room. Her irritation at her sister evaporated as she thought about how much better she would feel sitting on Cassie's bed with her. But when she reached Cassie's room, the door was closed. And when she tried to turn the knob, it didn't open.

That was weird. All the doors in the house had old-fashioned locks on them, the kind that opened with skeleton keys. But the agent who sold them the house hadn't had the keys, and they'd yet to find them anywhere in the house, so the doors were never locked. Not that they needed to lock them anyway.

But now, somehow, Cassie's door *was* locked.

Ava was about to knock on it and call out her sister's name when she heard something that sounded like voices coming from behind the door. Or at least one voice. Then there was a little laugh.

Even though the lights were out, a faint glow was visible through the keyhole. Ava knelt on the carpet in the hallway and peered through the small hole. Cassie was sitting on the floor next to the wall. She had a flashlight in her hand, and the light formed a circle around her.

Of course she's prepared for an emergency, Ava thought.

The thought almost made her laugh. Then Cassie shifted the flashlight and illuminated the spot on the wall where the crudely drawn figure of Rosemary was. Seeing the picture, Ava felt a shiver run down her back. It was even creepier than she'd remembered. The wild hair and the circle that was meant to be a mouth were ugly. The two black eyes stared back at Ava as if they could see her peeping through the keyhole.

Cassie said something that Ava couldn't make out. She laughed again. Then Cassie's head twisted around so that she was staring directly at the door. Ava gasped when she saw the angry expression on her sister's face. It reminded her of the one Rosemary had on hers. Even worse, her eyes were just as black and empty.

"Who's there?" Cassie said, her voice sharp. It didn't even sound like her.

Ava didn't know what to do. She didn't want Cassie to know she'd been spying on her. And what was Cassie doing in there anyway? There was something very weird about the way she was talking to herself. *Or maybe she's not talking to herself,* Ava thought as a horrible idea occurred to her. *Maybe she's talking to Rosemary.*

Cassie stood and walked toward the door. Ava got up and ran down the hall, the carpet thankfully muffling the sound of her footsteps. She reached her bedroom and slipped inside just as Cassie's bedroom door opened and the flashlight beam swept back and forth down the empty corridor. Ava stood inside her own room, her heart pounding.

The lights in her room came on suddenly, and she gave a little shriek of surprise. She stuck her head into the hallway and saw her mother standing at the top of the stairs. Farther down, Cassie was also in the hallway. Her arms were folded over her chest, and she was staring at Ava.

"Are you girls all right?" their mother asked.

"Great," Ava said, trying to sound normal.

"Fine," Cassie said. She was still watching her sister.

"I don't know what happened," their mother said. "We weren't running any power tools or anything like that. Were either of you using a hair dryer or something that might have overloaded the wiring?"

"Nope," Ava said. "I was just reading."

"Me neither," said Cassie.

"Okay," said their mother. "Well, everything is working now." She sighed. "I guess this old house has bad moods sometimes, just like the rest of us. I'd better go back down and make sure your father isn't accidentally rewiring a light switch to turn on the washing machine or something. Good night."

"Good night," Ava said.

Even after their mother left, Cassie continued to stand in the hallway.

"You okay?" Ava asked.

"Why wouldn't I be?" said Cassie. Then she grinned. "I'm not the one who's afraid of the dark." She waited a moment, then turned and went back into her room. Ava heard the door shut. She wondered, if she went and tried to turn the knob, if it would be locked again.

She went into her own room and shut the door. She tried not to think about what she'd seen through the keyhole in Cassie's door, but it was all she *could* think about. What had she been doing in there? It was almost as if she had been talking to Rosemary. But Rosemary was just a drawing. A creepy drawing, but still just a drawing. It wasn't like she was real.

She was probably just playing one of her games, Ava told herself. *Like when she had that imaginary friend when we were little.*

That was it. Cassie was just pretending. She'd always

liked making up stories. Sometimes, when they'd shared a room, she'd spent hours telling Ava about the adventures of the characters she invented. This was probably the same thing. And she had just been teasing Ava about being afraid of the dark. It was what sisters did sometimes.

By the time she'd gotten ready for bed, Ava felt better about everything. She'd just scared herself imagining things when the lights went out. There was nothing to be afraid of. It was just an old house, with old wiring. Still, as she slipped under the covers and laid her head on the pillow, she left the bedside table light on.

Just in case.

5

"That was excellent, Aisha."

Aisha grinned and bounced on her toes as Mrs. Randall, seated at the piano, looked around. "Who's next?" the music teacher asked. She nodded at Ava. "How about you?"

Ava shook her head. "Someone else can go," she said quickly. "I, um, haven't learned all the words yet."

"They're printed right there on the paper," Beth-Ann Jennings said. She and the girls standing around her laughed.

Auditions for the school musical had been going on for half an hour. Ava had been hoping that maybe she could hide in the group and not have to sing. Especially after she'd heard how good some of the other kids were. But now almost everyone had taken a turn.

"I'll go," Cassie said.

Ava gave her sister a thankful look. She had forgotten all about Cassie's strange behavior from the night before. And if Cassie had been upset with her about something, she had gotten over it, because things had been normal ever since breakfast. Neither of them had mentioned the cassette tape they'd found to Gwen or Aisha, and Ava had decided not to. Their house already had a reputation for being weird. It was probably better not to make things worse.

Mrs. Randall began playing, and Cassie started to sing. Ava had heard her sing before, of course, but she was surprised at how good Cassie sounded. She didn't seem to be nervous at all. Even Beth-Ann seemed reluctantly impressed, shrugging and nodding when one of her friends whispered something in her ear.

"Wow," Aisha said when the song ended. "That was great."

"Thanks," Cassie said. "It wasn't as good as yours, though."

"I think that just leaves you," Mrs. Randall said to Ava. "Are you ready to give it a try?"

Ava was not ready, but she nodded. Mrs. Randall began to play.

"You can do it," Cassie said softly.

When the time came for Ava to start singing, though, she completely forgot the first word. She stumbled over the lyrics, even though they were right in front of her. Beth-Ann and her friends laughed, and Ava wished she could disappear.

Mrs. Randall stopped. "Let's try that again," she said kindly. "Whenever you're ready."

Ava took a deep breath. She concentrated on the paper in her hand, trying to block out everything else. *Just get it over with*, she told herself. She nodded at Mrs. Randall.

The teacher had played only a few notes when the lights in the room flickered on and off. Mrs. Randall kept going, but the flickering grew more intense, the lights flashing repeatedly. They kept doing it even after Mrs. Randall stopped playing.

"What in the world?" she said.

"It's just like last night," Ava said to herself. She looked at Cassie, who was staring up at the lights with a peculiar expression. Her lips were moving silently, and it looked to Ava as if she was saying, "Stop it, stop it, stop it."

The lights continued to flash.

"Perhaps we should move to another room," Mrs. Randall said, standing up. "Follow me, please."

She left the classroom and went down the hall to the school's auditorium, the students following along behind her. There, the Drama Club advisor, Mr. Chowdry, stood near the stage that ran across one end of the room.

"All finished with the singing auditions?" he asked Mrs. Randall.

"For the moment," Mrs. Randall answered. She looked up at the ceiling. "Any trouble with the lights in here?"

"No," Mr. Chowdry said. "Why?"

"Something's wrong with the power in my room," said Mrs. Randall. "I'm going to go down to the maintenance office and see if Ms. Gillikson will come take a look, if you don't mind starting the acting auditions."

"Not at all," Mr. Chowdry said.

He picked up a pile of scripts and started handing them out. Ava, relieved to have gotten out of having to sing in front of everyone, took one. So did Cassie and Aisha.

"That thing with the lights was weird," Aisha remarked.

"Probably just some bad wiring," said Cassie. "It happens at our house a lot."

"I can't remember it ever happening before," Aisha said. "And right in the middle of your audition too," she added. "Weird," she said again.

Ava flipped through the pages of the script, hoping

Aisha would stop talking about the lights. Fortunately, Mr. Chowdry came to her rescue.

"The audition scene is on page twelve," he said. "You won't have time to memorize it, but read it over and familiarize yourselves with your lines. Gentlemen, you'll be reading the part of the Woodsman. Ladies, you'll be reading the part of the Witch."

"Isn't that kind of sexist?" Beth-Ann said. "Girls can cut down trees too, you know."

"Right," agreed a boy behind her. "And guys can be witches if we want to."

"Good points," said Mr. Chowdry. He looked around, his finger moving up and down as he counted heads. "Tell you what. We need an even number of witches and woodsmen, so everybody on this side of the room"—he pointed to the left—"are woodsmen. And everybody on this side"—he pointed to the right—"are witches. How's that sound?"

There were a couple of groans on both sides, but nobody asked to switch.

"Excellent," said Mr. Chowdry. "You've got fifteen minutes to go over your lines. Then I'll call up one witch and one woodsman at a time to read."

Ava, Cassie, and Aisha, all of whom happened to be on the witch side of the room, went and sat down in a row at the front. Ava opened her script and looked at the lines.

"Do you think this is the actual show we're doing?" said Cassie, who was sitting in the middle.

Aisha shook her head. "They announce what we're really doing once everyone has auditioned," she said. "They think having us read from a different script means no one has an advantage. Like, if this was a scene from *Seussical*, I'd have all my lines memorized already."

"You'd probably have *everyone's* lines memorized already," Cassie joked.

Aisha laughed. "It's true," she said. "I really hope that *is* the show we're doing."

Loud laughter interrupted them. Ava looked over and saw Beth-Ann and her friends a few rows behind theirs.

They didn't seem to be paying any attention to their scripts at all.

"Doesn't she think she has to practice?" Ava said.

Aisha snorted. "She thinks she's a fantastic actress," she said. "Just because she was on that one show. She didn't even have any lines."

"Ignore her," Cassie said. "She's nothing."

There was an angry tone to her sister's voice that surprised Ava. Cassie was usually never competitive unless it was about grades. Not even about video games. Ava was the one who hated to lose. She looked at Cassie's face. She was still looking at Beth-Ann and her friends and scowling fiercely. She really did look like an angry witch.

"Ten minutes!" Mr. Chowdry called out. "Ten minutes until we start auditions."

Ava returned her attention to the script. The scene was about the Woodsman arriving at the Witch's cottage. He was looking for two lost children and wanted to know if the Witch was hiding them inside. She was, but she didn't want him to know that. The dialogue was actually very funny, and Ava was giggling when Mr. Chowdry called for the first two people to go up onstage.

"Our first Woodsman will be Beth-Ann," he said, "since she seems to be done studying her lines."

Beth-Ann jumped up and walked toward the stage. She seemed confident, as if auditioning was just a formality and she already had the lead.

"And our first Witch will be—"

"I'll go," Cassie said, standing up.

Mr. Chowdry seemed surprised. "Well, okay," he said.

Cassie started walking away.

"You forgot your script," Aisha called out.

"I don't need it," Cassie said as she walked up the steps on one side of the stage and went to stand in front of Beth-Ann.

Ava watched as the two of them began their scene.

"Why are you rapping on my door, interrupting my

dinner?" Cassie asked, her voice creaky as if she were a very old woman.

"A good question," Beth-Ann said. "And here's another one—what are you *having* for dinner? It wouldn't by any chance be the two children who are lost in this forest, would it?"

Cassie made a sound like she was horrified by the thought. "What do I want with scrawny children?" she said. "Especially since I'm a vegetarian."

Mr. Chowdry laughed as Beth-Ann looked confused. "That's not in the script," she said.

"Script?" said Cassie. "What do you think this is, Woodsman, some kind of detective show? If so, you'd best learn your lines."

Everyone in the auditorium laughed as Beth-Ann, fuming, put her hands on her hips. "You didn't say we were going to ad-lib!" she wailed.

"Okay," Mr. Chowdry said. "Cassie, that's very good. But let's do the scene as written now."

Cassie nodded. Beth-Ann started over, and this time Cassie delivered the lines exactly as they were written. But even saying the words just as they appeared on the page, she somehow made her Witch feel alive, while Beth-Ann's Woodsman was boring, as if Beth-Ann were reading the list of ingredients off a cereal box. When they finished, Beth-Ann stomped down the stairs, while Cassie walked back to her seat with a grin on her face.

"That was fantastic," Aisha told her.

"It sure was," Ava agreed.

"I don't know where it came from," said Cassie. "It's like I opened my mouth and the words just fell out. I don't even remember what I said."

Aisha sighed. "That's real acting," she said.

They sat and watched the remaining pairs run through the scene. Aisha was fantastic, as Ava had expected her to be. When it was her own turn, she did a fine but unremarkable job, and felt relieved when it was over.

"Okay," Mr. Chowdry said when the last pair had

performed. "Tonight, Mrs. Randall and I will get together and discuss your two auditions. Tomorrow morning, a cast list will be posted on the music room door."

"What's the show going to be?" Aisha asked.

"Tomorrow," Mr. Chowdry said.

Aisha groaned. As the girls picked up their things to walk to the school bus, she said, "Ava, you didn't get to do your singing audition. You should talk to Mrs. Randall about that."

"It's okay," Ava said. "I don't expect to get a part. Not a big one, anyway."

"I'm sure Cassie will," Aisha said. "And I hope it's one that Beth-Ann really wanted."

Cassie laughed. Ava, walking beside her, was happy for her. But she also felt a little uneasy, the way she had the night before when she'd seen Cassie through the keyhole. It was like her familiar sister had become someone else for a moment.

"Maybe we'll have something to celebrate on Saturday

in addition to having the first meeting of our book club," Aisha said. "That reminds me. The books will be here tomorrow. I know that doesn't give us a lot of time to read it, but we can talk about the chapters we do get through. Besides, this is more about having fun. I can't wait to see your house."

"We're going to have a great time," Cassie agreed.

"Yeah," Ava said. "Great."

She wished she were as excited about the sleepover as she was pretending to be. But maybe it *would* be fun. She just hoped nothing weird happened.

6

When they arrived home from school, the garden looked very different.

"Wow," Ava said when she saw what her parents had gotten done. "It doesn't look like a jungle anymore."

"Well, a little bit less like a jungle," her father said. He was surrounded by big paper lawn-waste bags filled with chopped-up pieces of rosebushes. "But now we can get inside the summerhouse. Come take a look."

Ava walked excitedly up the now-cleared path to the small house at the center of the garden. Cassie, however, hung back.

"Don't you want to see what it looks like in there?" her mother asked.

"Maybe later," Cassie said. "I have some homework to do."

She went up the steps and disappeared into the big house.

"Did she have a bad day at school?" said Ava's father.

"No," Ava answered. "Actually, I think she might have landed a lead in the school musical."

She didn't know why her sister wasn't interested in exploring the summerhouse. She, however, couldn't wait to get inside. Ava opened the door and stepped in.

"It's still a wreck," her mother said. "But I think we'll be able to turn it into something really nice."

Although on the outside the summerhouse looked like a smaller version of the main house, inside it was mostly one big room.

"It's almost like a dollhouse version of our house," Ava remarked.

Against one wall of the room were two beds. The metal frames were covered in peeling white paint, and the handmade quilts that covered the mattresses were faded and moth-eaten. Between the beds was a small bookcase. It had glass-paned doors, behind which were two shelves of books. An empty oil lamp sat on top, along with a small, round china plate with a pattern of roses on it. In the center of the plate rested a dead spider, its dried-up legs curled under it.

"This would have been a lovely place to sleep in the summer," Ava's mother said. "Just imagine what it would have been like with all the windows open and the smell of the roses coming in."

Ava, crouching down, opened the doors of the bookcase and examined the books inside. They all seemed to be fairy-tale collections. She took one out and opened the cover. Inside, written in black ink, was *For Violet and Lily, on their very special day. From Mother and Father.* Ava thought about the photograph they'd found of the two girls. *They must have been sisters*, she thought, pleased to have solved the mystery.

She flipped through the book, which contained lots of beautiful color illustrations. She couldn't wait to show it to Cassie. It was exactly the kind of book she loved. Also, she would be excited that they had another clue to who Lily and Violet were.

"Tomorrow I'll wash these windows and see what it looks like with lots of sunlight shining in," Ava's father said. "Some new paint and a few repairs to the roof, and this place will be fantastic."

He sounded excited. Ava, looking around at the dusty floors and water-stained walls, also found herself imagining what the summerhouse could look like. Until now, she hadn't been able to think of Blackthorn House as anything but a run-down mess that was taking up all their time and attention and, worse, had taken her away from her friends and her old life. She still didn't feel like it was home, and things could be better at school—way better— but now she was starting to see what the house might become.

"We need to run to the hardware store," her father said. "Do you want to come?"

"No thanks," Ava said. "I'm going to look around a little more."

"Okay," said her mother. "Just watch out for rusty nails or anything you could get cut on."

Ava laughed. "If I promise not to play with any old knives or broken glass, will you bring back pizza for dinner?"

"Deal," her mother replied.

Her parents left, and Ava resumed looking around the summerhouse. There wasn't really a whole lot to explore, and it didn't take her long to see everything. When she was done, she sat down on one of the two beds. The springs groaned. Then Ava realized that there was something under the quilt. She stood up and pulled it back.

The thing she'd sat on was actually under the mattress. When Ava lifted it up, she discovered a book, small and bound in leather. Only when she opened it, she found that it wasn't a book at all. It was a diary. She looked at the first page.

June 21st, 1916

I am worried about Violet. She has not been herself. Several times at night I have been awakened by the sound of her whispering, as if talking to someone. But never is there anyone there, and she says I must be dreaming. At first I thought perhaps she was right. But last night I only pretended to sleep, and shortly thereafter the whispering began as before. I could not understand most of what she said, but I did hear her say a name—Rosemary. I don't know who this could be, as we know nobody by this name and no one comes here to the house due to the presence of the fever. Perhaps it is Violet who is talking in her sleep. I am not sure what to do next.

Ava felt the room grow cold around her. She looked up, half expecting to see that clouds were blocking the sun from coming in. But the same warm light slipped through the grimy windows, and through the open door she saw the bright, clear September afternoon. Nothing had changed.

She stared at the diary page, rereading the words written more than a hundred years earlier. She assumed the writer was Lily Blackthorn. But what she'd written could almost have been written by Ava herself. That Lily had mentioned the name "Rosemary" was especially weird. When she'd seen the drawing on Cassie's wall, Ava had assumed that Rosemary must have been someone who lived in the house at one time. But if Lily had never heard of her, who was she?

Maybe it's not the same Rosemary, Ava thought.

But what were the chances of there being two?

She was about to flip through more of the diary when a shadow appeared in the doorway.

"What are you doing?" Cassie asked.

Ava quickly slid the book behind her on the bed, although she wasn't sure why she felt it was important to hide the diary from her sister. "Nothing," she said.

Cassie looked around the room but didn't step inside. "It smells weird in here," she said. "It's probably filled with mold. You shouldn't sit there too long, or you might breathe it in."

"I wouldn't want to do that," Ava said.

"I wish your father would just tear this down," Cassie said.

"My father?" said Ava. "You mean *Dad*?"

Cassie looked confused for a second. Then she laughed. "Of course," she said. "I was just being funny."

"Right," said Ava, pretending to laugh a little bit too. "Good one."

"Anyway, I'm going back inside," Cassie said. "Are you coming?"

Ava could tell that Cassie really wanted her to leave

the summerhouse. Why? And why had she showed up right after Ava had discovered Lily Blackthorn's diary? She felt like these things were connected, but she couldn't see how.

Cassie was watching her expectantly, waiting for an answer.

"Sure," Ava said. "I just want to bring some of these cool books I found."

She opened the doors on the bookcase and pretended to peruse the titles. Picking three at random, she brought them out and set them on the bed, on top of the diary. Then she picked up all four.

"What are those?" Cassie asked her.

"Just some old books," Ava said. "They have some neat illustrations in them that I think you'll like."

Cassie looked at the books and shrugged. Then she turned and walked back toward the house. Ava walked beside her, holding the books to her chest. When they got inside, Ava went upstairs to her room. She slipped the diary beneath her mattress, just as Lily Blackthorn had. The other books she left on her bedside table, so she could show them to Cassie later. Then she went back downstairs. Cassie was in the kitchen, opening and closing the drawers in the cabinets. When Ava came in, she stopped.

"Looking for something?" Ava asked her.

Cassie shook her head. "A pen," she said. "But I remembered I have one upstairs."

Ava knew her twin wasn't telling the truth. For one thing, there were pens all over the place. Ava could see three of them lying on the counter. Cassie wouldn't have to hunt through drawers to find one. For another, Cassie seemed nervous, as if she'd been caught. She'd been looking for something, all right, but it wasn't a pen.

Ava decided not to say anything about it. After all, she was hiding her own secret upstairs. Still, it bothered her that she and her sister were keeping things from each other. They almost never did that. Lately, though, it felt like there were more and more things they weren't sharing. Like they were growing apart.

The door opened and their parents came in. Their mother carried two pizza boxes, and the scent of cheese and pepperoni filled the air. Behind her, their father held up a bag.

"We got ice cream too," he said. "To celebrate."

"Celebrate what?" Cassie asked.

"You getting a part in the school musical," her father said.

Cassie gave Ava a look. "You told them?"

"I said you *probably* got a part," Ava said.

Cassie groaned. "That's bad luck," she said. "You're not supposed to talk about it until it's official."

"I'm sure it will be fine," their mother said, opening the lids of the pizza boxes.

"Right," said their father. "Especially if you eat a big bowl of ice cream. Everyone knows that counteracts any bad luck."

"Maybe," Cassie said, sounding unsure. "But I think I also need to eat *three* slices of pizza to make sure. I'm pretty sure those are the rules."

"You might want to make it four," said Ava in a serious tone. "You don't want to take any chances."

Cassie laughed, and this time it sounded like her real laugh. Ava laughed too. Maybe everything was fine, and she was just thinking too much. *You need to relax*, she told herself as she picked up a slice of pizza and took a bite.

Then she remembered the diary hidden in her bedroom. *I am not sure what to do next.* She heard the words aloud in her head, spoken in a girl's voice from a century before. Lily Blackthorn had been worried about her sister too. Why?

Ava took another bite. She would worry about that later. Right now, she had pizza to eat.

7

The crowd around the door to Mrs. Randall's room was so thick that Ava, Cassie, Aisha, and Gwen couldn't even see the paper taped to the glass.

"Glinda?" Beth-Ann Jennings sounded angry. "She only gets *one* stupid song."

She turned and pushed through the crowd. As she passed by Ava and her friends, she said, "Congratulations, Dorothy" in a sarcastic tone.

"I guess we're doing *The Wizard of Oz*," Aisha said. "But which one of us is Dorothy?"

The group of kids dispersed as people saw which roles,

if any, they would be playing. Some were excited, while others seemed upset. Finally, Gwen elbowed her way through the remaining kids so that they could see the cast list for themselves.

"It's Aisha," she said. "And Cassie is the Scarecrow."

"What about Ava?" Cassie asked, scanning the list until she found her sister's name. "Oh."

"'Oh' what?" Ava asked.

"Flying Monkey," Cassie told her.

"Hey, at least you all got parts," said Gwen. "That's great."

"And we'll be in most of the scenes together," Aisha added. "Well, Cassie and I will," she added, sounding a little bit apologetic.

"It's okay, you guys," Ava said. "I didn't expect to get a part at all. I didn't even sing, remember? Besides, I'm a Flying Monkey. I get to *fly*. You guys have to *walk* down the Yellow Brick Road."

"I'm surprised they didn't cast Beth-Ann as the Wicked

Witch of the West," Gwen said, snorting. "She'd be perfect for that."

The others laughed as they walked in the direction of their homerooms. Ava really didn't care that she hadn't gotten one of the main roles. And she was happy for Cassie that she had gotten one of the leads.

"Let's stop at the library and pick up our copies of *Sisters in Time*," Aisha suggested. "We've got enough time before the bell."

They made a short detour down a hallway and through the library doors. Walking up to the desk, Aisha greeted the man standing behind it. "Hey, Mr. Monday," she said. "Did those books come in?"

"They did," the librarian replied, reaching under the desk and bringing out a stack of four books. "Here you go. And you might be interested to know that Taraji Lang, the author of that book, is going to be here next week to talk to us."

"Really?" Aisha said. "Here? Like, right *here* at Patience Prufrock Central School?"

Mr. Monday laughed. "You sound surprised."

"I am," Aisha said. "A real live author coming here? That's a big deal. Now I'm going to have to read *all* her books before her visit."

"If anyone can, Aisha, it's you," said Mr. Monday. "Now you all better get to class. The bell's about to ring."

Aisha handed each of them a copy of *Sisters in Time*, then they left the library and headed to their homerooms, arriving just as the bell started clanging. The room was buzzing with voices as everyone talked about the posting of the cast list for the musical, and several people congratulated Aisha and Cassie on landing the leads.

"Of course, my costume is going to be *spectacular*," Beth-Ann said loudly. "The costume designer who works with my uncle is going to make it. He made the dress that Simone Galvant wore to the Academy Awards."

Ava tuned Beth-Ann out. Why did she always have to be the center of attention? It was so annoying. If anyone should be bragging right now, it was Aisha. Or Cassie. Ava knew her sister was thrilled that she was going to be the Scarecrow. He was one of her favorite characters in the Oz books.

"I'm so glad I'm not something stupid, like a Flying Monkey."

Beth-Ann's comment cut through Ava's happy thoughts. She felt herself tense up. She really wanted to tell Beth-Ann to shut up, but she knew that would just make things worse.

Cassie turned to look at Beth-Ann. "You'd better watch out," she said, "or someone might just drop a house on you."

Beth-Ann's mouth fell open as the class erupted in laughter. "That's not even the right witch," she sputtered. But it didn't matter. Everyone was laughing at her.

Cassie turned back around, a satisfied grin on her face. Ava didn't know what to say. It was such an un-Cassie thing to do. She wasn't sure if she was impressed or shocked. Then Ms. Gonnick told them all to quiet down so she could take attendance, and it was over.

Except that it wasn't.

All morning, everywhere they went, kids teased Beth-Ann about being a witch. They asked her where her magic wand was. They pretended to be Munchkins and talked about her in funny voices. They asked her if she and the Wicked Witch of the West were best friends. By the time fourth period came and the girls headed for the gymnasium for PE, Beth-Ann was good and mad. And she was especially mad at Cassie.

When the gym teacher, Ms. Calfstock, told them that they would be going outside to play soccer, Ava was thrilled. The weather was warm and sunny, and she couldn't wait to get on the field. It wasn't quite the same as practicing with the team, or playing a real game, but at least she was going to kick a ball around for a while.

At their old school, Ava had always been chosen as a team captain. Then she always chose Cassie first to be on her team, so she could help her out and make sure she didn't mess up too badly. But here, nobody knew how good she was. Besides, Ms. Calfstock broke them into teams by having them count off. The even-numbered girls were on one team, and the odd-numbered girls on the other. Because Ava and Cassie were standing next to each other when they counted, it meant they were separated. But Cassie was on a team with Gwen and Aisha, so at first Ava thought things would be okay.

Then she realized that *she* was on a team with Beth-Ann.

That part wasn't so bad. As teammates, they had to work together if they wanted to win. And it turned out that Beth-Ann liked to win almost as much as Ava did. The problem was, every time Beth-Ann got the ball, she headed directly toward Cassie. Poor Cassie, who was supposed to be playing fullback, looked terrified whenever Beth-Ann came running at her. Ava couldn't do anything but watch as Cassie attempted to stop Beth-Ann and failed, either kicking helplessly at the ball or ending up flat on her face in the grass as Beth-Ann dashed by and kicked the ball into the goal.

After the third time Beth-Ann steamrollered over Cassie, Ava ran over to help her sister up. "You've got to at least *try* to stop her," she said. "When she comes at you, kick the ball away from her."

"I don't think I can," Cassie said, trying to wipe the grass stains off her knees.

"Sure you can," Ava said, trying to sound confident. "Just pretend she's got Toto and you need to snatch him away from her."

Cassie smiled weakly and nodded. "I'll try," she said.

The ball went back into play. Again, it ended up getting passed to Beth-Ann. And again, she headed right for Cassie. She had a wicked grin on her face as she powered down the field. Ava looked at Cassie, who seemed like she might throw up. She bent her knees and held out her hands, as if she was trying to cast some kind of spell to ward off the approaching Beth-Ann.

Ava groaned and waited for her sister to get flattened again. But just as Beth-Ann was about to bang into Cassie, something happened. Beth-Ann was knocked off her feet and went flying backward through the air, as if some powerful force had hit her in the stomach. She landed on her back, and the ball she'd been kicking went rolling away.

Cassie was still crouched down with her hands out. Anyone watching might have thought she was the one who had sent Beth-Ann flying. But that was impossible. For one thing, she hadn't moved. For another, there was just no way she could have pushed Beth-Ann that hard.

Beth-Ann, though, thought that she had. Once she caught her breath, she jumped to her feet and started shouting. "Did you see that?" she yelled. "Did you see what she did? Ms. Calfstock, that's a foul! I get a penalty kick!"

"I didn't do anything!" Cassie protested. "I don't know what happened."

Beth-Ann charged at her. Immediately, she was

surrounded by a bunch of girls, holding her back. Ava ran over to her sister and stood in front of her, her arms across her chest as she stared down Beth-Ann.

"What are you going to do?" Beth-Ann sneered. "Drop a house on me?"

"No, but I might try throwing a bucket of water on you and seeing if you melt," Ava snapped back.

"Okay, okay," said Ms. Calfstock. "That's enough. Beth-Ann, are you hurt?"

"No," Beth-Ann admitted. "But I *could* have been."

"Cassie didn't do anything," Ava said.

"She had to have," Beth-Ann said. "I didn't just—"

"Enough," Ms. Calfstock said. "The period is about over, anyway. Everybody go change."

The girls wandered off, Beth-Ann surrounded by her friends, some of whom looked back at Cassie and gave her nasty glares. Gwen and Aisha joined Ava and Cassie.

"I know you didn't hit her," Gwen said to Cassie. "But what *did* happen?"

Cassie shook her head. "I don't know," she said. "One second Beth-Ann was running at me, and I was wishing I knew what to do. The next, she was in the air. I have no idea how it happened."

Gwen looked at Ava, who shrugged. "Beth-Ann says she's a great actress," she said. "Maybe she just gave the performance of the year."

"Maybe," Gwen said, but she sounded doubtful.

There was an awkward silence. Then Aisha said, "We should go in."

The four of them walked together, not saying anything. But Ava could tell that Gwen and Aisha weren't convinced that what had happened was an accident.

Neither was she.

8

"My favorite part of the book is when Imani goes through the mirror and stops the killer from—"

"Hold up!" Gwen interrupted. "Some of us haven't finished it yet."

Aisha groaned. "But it's so good," she said. "I want to talk about it."

"I finished it too," said Cassie. "You and I can talk about it later."

Aisha took a slice of pizza from the box on the floor. "This is so much fun," she said. "My mother never lets us order pizza. We should have book-group sleepovers every weekend."

The four girls were in the summerhouse. Ava and Cassie had spent all morning sweeping it out and getting it ready. Now they had their sleeping bags spread out in a circle on the floor. Three battery-powered camp lanterns filled the room with light, and the weather was still warm enough that they could stay out there without getting too cold. The only inconvenient part was that they had to go inside to use the bathroom, but that wasn't a big deal.

"So, what do you guys think of Blackthorn House?" Ava asked. "Is it as scary as you thought it would be?"

"Nah," said Gwen. "It's just a big old house."

"It is a little creepy," Aisha said. "But in a fun way. I'm still going to tell Bobby Endicott that we saw the ghost, though."

"You haven't had anything happen since you moved in?" asked Gwen. "No weird sounds? No doors opening and closing by themselves? Nothing?"

Ava looked over at Cassie. She waited to see if her sister

would say anything about the lights, or maybe about the drawing on her wall. When they'd given Aisha and Gwen a tour of the house, there had been a big stuffed rabbit sitting on the floor in Cassie's room covering the picture of Rosemary.

"No," Ava said when Cassie didn't reply. "I guess the ghosts moved out when we moved in."

"Actually," Cassie said, "we did find one weird thing."

Ava, surprised, looked at her sister. Cassie had a funny smile on her face, as if she'd been keeping a secret.

"What?" Gwen asked.

Cassie reached into her backpack, which was on the floor beside her sleeping bag, and pulled something out. "This," she said.

Ava gasped. Cassie was holding the cassette tape they'd found behind the wall. The one their mother wouldn't let them listen to. "Where did you get that?"

"Where Mom hid it," Cassie said.

"What is it?" asked Aisha.

"A recording of a séance," Cassie said. "Well, we think that's what it is. We've only heard the first part."

"A séance?" said Gwen, sounding skeptical. "Like to talk to dead people?"

Cassie nodded. "Held here in the house. To contact the spirit of Violet Blackthorn. She was Lily Blackthorn's sister. So, do you want to hear it?"

Aisha and Gwen looked at each other. "Yes!" they said in unison.

"I don't know, Cassie," Ava said cautiously. "Mom doesn't want us—"

"You're the one who wanted to hear it," said Cassie, cutting her off. "Remember?"

Ava nodded. "Yeah," she said. "But . . ."

"But what?" said Cassie when Ava didn't finish the sentence.

Ava, who was thinking about Lily Blackthorn's diary—which she still had not told Cassie about finding and had been too freaked out to read any more of—wasn't sure what to say. She had been the one who wanted to hear what was on the tape. And she still did. But she couldn't help thinking about what Lily had written about her sister behaving strangely. She also couldn't help thinking that Cassie had been behaving a little strangely too. She couldn't say that, though.

"You're right," she said, trying to sound enthusiastic while also quickly thinking of an excuse that might solve the whole problem. "How are we going to play it, though? We'd have to go back in the house, and Mom and Dad are still up."

Cassie got up and walked over to one of the beds. "I already thought of that," she said, kneeling down and reaching underneath. She pulled out the boom box their father had found. "And you can run it on batteries, so we don't need electricity," she continued, looking at Ava as if she'd known her twin would bring that up next.

"I guess you thought of everything," Ava said as Cassie brought the boom box over and set it down in the center of the circle made by their sleeping bags.

Cassie popped open the compartment where the tape went, put it in, and closed it again. "Ready?" she said.

The others nodded. Cassie pushed the button to start the tape.

As before, a woman began to speak. "This is the night of Wednesday, September thirteenth, 1978," she said. "It is the anniversary of the death of Violet Blackthorn, and we are here to communicate with her spirit."

Unlike the last time, nobody objected and stopped the tape, and the woman continued. "Everyone, please join hands," she said. "Our connection to one another will create a powerful circle of energy that will attract the spirit and contain it."

There was a rustling sound. Then the woman spoke again. "I call upon the spirit of Violet Blackthorn," she said in a firm voice. "I invite you into our circle. Please, join us."

There was a long period of silence. The tape hissed slightly, but no one spoke.

"Is anything happening?" Gwen asked impatiently.

"Shh," Aisha said. "They're waiting."

"She's here!" a woman's voice said, causing the girls to squeak in fright.

"That's a different voice," Aisha said.

"My sister is here," the same voice said. "I feel her presence. Violet? It's Lily. Do you hear me?"

There was a thumping sound, followed by two more. It sounded like someone knocking on a door.

"She's trying to come through," said the voice of the first woman. "Something is holding her back."

"Violet!" cried Lily Blackthorn. "Violet, come into the circle!"

There was more thumping. Several voices spoke at once, sounding afraid.

"What is that?" said a man's voice.

There was a loud crash, and the sound of glass shattering. Lots of people spoke at once.

"Don't break the circle!" the first woman said sternly.

"It isn't Violet." Lily Blackthorn's voice was shaky as she spoke. "It isn't my sister."

"Who is it?" a man asked, sounding panicked. "Who?"

There was more knocking, as if the spirit trying to get through was trying to break down a door.

"Rosemary," Lily said, her voice barely a whisper.

A loud crackling sound filled the air. Then the tape stopped. Cassie pushed the button to make it play, but nothing happened.

"I guess that's it," Gwen said.

"That was weird," said Aisha. "And really creepy."

"Just sounded like a lot of banging to me," said Gwen, but Ava had a feeling she was trying to seem braver than she probably felt.

"If Violet is Lily's sister, then who's that Rosemary person she talked about?" Aisha asked.

Once again, Ava waited to see if Cassie would say anything. This time, she did. "Probably someone else who lived in this house once," she said.

"Whoever she is, Lily sounded afraid of her," said Aisha. "Like she really didn't want her showing up."

Cassie looked annoyed by that comment. "She was probably just upset that her sister didn't want to talk to her," she said.

"Maybe," said Aisha. "But what about all that banging? And why did everybody sound so scared?"

"It's probably all fake anyway," said Cassie. "I mean, does anybody believe in things like ghosts and talking to dead people?"

"I do," Gwen said instantly. "I believe in all of it. Ghosts. Aliens. Bigfoot. And I think something really scary was going on there. Where did you find that tape?"

"Inside one of the walls," Ava said when Cassie didn't answer.

"Also scary," said Gwen. "Like the spirits hid it there for you to find."

"There was all kinds of stuff in there," Cassie said. "It's no big deal. What do you guys want to do now?"

It was obvious to Ava that Cassie was trying to change the subject. But why? She was the one who wanted to listen to the tape so badly that she'd taken it from wherever their mother had hidden it. Now she sounded like she didn't want to talk about it anymore.

"I brought a card game," Aisha said. "Unicorns and Zombies. Want to play?"

"Definitely," Gwen said.

"Sure," Ava added.

Cassie shrugged. "Sure," she echoed.

Aisha took the game out and started explaining it to them. Pretty soon, they all seemed to forget about the tape and what was on it. Then they played three rounds of the game, which ended with Gwen's unicorn army defeating the rest of them.

"Wow, it's after midnight," Aisha said, yawning. "I think it's time to get some sleep."

They all crawled into their sleeping bags. But despite what Aisha said, they didn't go to sleep right away. They kept on talking. Eventually, though, one by one they drifted off.

When Ava woke up, for a moment she couldn't figure out where she was. Then she remembered. The summerhouse. But what had woken her up? She lay in the darkness, listening, but all she heard was Gwen snoring and the other two breathing. She closed her eyes and tried to go back to sleep, but something kept nagging at her, some sense that they weren't alone in the summerhouse.

She opened her eyes again, sat up, and looked around. The moon shining through the windows made a bright line across the room. She followed the light to where it ended at one of the beds. Her heart froze in her chest as—just for a moment—she saw the shadow of a girl sitting on the edge of the bed, looking at her. Then the girl blinked out, like a light turning off, and there was nothing there.

You just imagined it, Ava told herself. *That tape put ideas into your head. There's nothing there.*

Then she smelled something. She sniffed, and the scent

of roses filled her nose, rich and fragrant. It was as if there were bushes blooming right outside the window.

But there are no roses right now, she thought. *Not one.*

She inhaled again, and again she smelled roses. It wasn't her imagination.

Something strange was definitely going on. But what? She wanted to wake the others and ask them if they could smell the roses too. But what if they couldn't? What if it was all in her head? She wasn't sure if that would be better or worse than them saying they could smell the flowers.

She pulled her sleeping bag up around her neck. She didn't know what time it was, but it had to be the middle of the night. She should try to go back to sleep. But something told her she was still going to be awake when the sun came up.

9

On Sunday morning, after a big breakfast of pancakes, Ava and Cassie's parents drove Gwen and Aisha home. Then they were going to the hardware store again, so the twins were left home alone. Ava, who was tired from barely getting any sleep the night before, wanted to escape to her room to rest. Instead, she decided it was time to have a talk with her twin.

"Hey," she said, standing in the doorway of Cassie's room. Her sister was on her bed, reading a book.

"Hey," Cassie said, without looking over or putting the book down.

"What are you doing?" Ava asked. "I mean, I see what you're doing. I guess what I mean is, can we talk?"

"Sure," Cassie said, closing the book and setting it on the bed beside her. "About what?"

Ava walked into the room and sat down on the edge of the bed. Glancing at the wall, she saw that the stuffed rabbit was still covering up the drawing of Rosemary. This made her feel slightly better, but not much, given what she was about to say.

"So, the thing with the tape was a little weird, huh?" she began.

"I guess," Cassie replied, shrugging.

"Who do you think Rosemary was?" Ava asked.

"No idea," said Cassie. "Probably just some girl they knew."

Ava nodded. "Probably," she said. She looked at the rabbit again. "Don't you think it's strange that there's a drawing of her on your wall, though?"

"Not really," Cassie answered. "Do you?"

Ava wasn't sure what to say. Her sister wasn't making this easy at all. But she really wanted to talk about what was going on, so she said, "I don't think what happened with Beth-Ann on the field was an accident. Or the lights going out at school. And I think there's something weird happening here in the house too."

Cassie laughed. "Weird how?" she said, as if Ava was being totally ridiculous.

"The lights," Ava said. "That tape. The way you—"

"The way I what?" said Cassie when Ava cut herself off.

Ava shook her head. "Never mind," she said. "I guess reading that book has made me think some strange things. That's all."

"No," Cassie said. "Finish what you were going to say. You think I'm acting weird?"

"No," Ava said. "Not weird, exactly."

"Then what?" Cassie pressed. She sounded a little angry now, and Ava wished she'd never said anything.

Ava shrugged. "I don't know," she said. She knew that

Cassie wouldn't let it go now that she'd brought it up. "Different, I guess. You've been acting different."

"And you don't like it," Cassie said. "You don't like that I'm the one getting attention for once."

"No," Ava said. But that wasn't entirely true. "It's not that you're getting attention."

"It's that you're *not*," said Cassie.

"That isn't what I mean!" Ava said, frustrated. Cassie was taking her words and turning them against her. "I don't care that you're making friends, or got a lead in the musical, or any of that. I'm *happy* for you. I just think there's something strange going on. That's all. First you find that"—she pointed to the wall—"then the thing with Beth-Ann. Then the name 'Rosemary' is mentioned on the tape of the séance. And in the—"

She stopped. She'd been about to tell Cassie about Lily Blackthorn's diary. But something told her to keep that to herself for a while longer. Instead, she said, "And I think I saw something in the summerhouse."

"Saw something?" Cassie said. "Like what?"

"I don't know," said Ava. "A shadow, I guess. But it looked like a girl. And I smelled roses."

"There are no roses right now," Cassie said.

"I know," said Ava. "Which is why it was weird."

"I didn't smell anything," Cassie said, as if that settled it. "Maybe the wind blew the scent in from someone else's garden. And you just said the thing you saw was probably a shadow. I don't know what you're so upset about."

"I'm not upset," said Ava. "I just thought we should talk about this."

"And now we have," said Cassie, picking up her book. "If you don't mind, I want to finish this. Then I have lines to memorize for our first practice tomorrow."

"Sure," Ava said, standing up. "I'll just go practice flapping my monkey wings."

"Have fun," Cassie said as Ava left the room.

That was a waste of time, Ava thought as she walked back

to her room. Cassie had more or less treated everything she had to say as a joke. *She never would have done that before.*

Before.

Before they moved into Blackthorn House.

Before they uncovered the drawing of Rosemary.

Before they found the photo of Lily and Violet.

Before they found the cassette.

Ava wished they could go back to before. But they couldn't. Blackthorn House was their home now. That meant she was going to have to figure out what, if anything, was going on. Part of her wanted to believe that nothing was. After all, almost everything that had happened could be reasonably explained. Even the incident with Beth-Ann during the soccer game could be Beth-Ann faking it to get attention.

She didn't believe that, though.

Back in her room, she shut the door, took Lily Blackthorn's diary out from its hiding place, and opened it. It was time to look for more clues.

June 30th, 1916

There is no moon tonight. The blackness surrounds the house like a cloak. It doesn't help that the rain that began this morning has not ceased even for a moment. Thunder rattles the windows like someone pounding on them with their fists, and everything feels cold and damp. Even the gas lights flicker weakly, as though they are afraid.

Violet has a fever. It came on this afternoon, as if the storm brought it. She is in her bed, wrapped in blankets. I have been forbidden to visit her, lest I too become ill. I can tell that everyone is worried.

I have come up to the angels' nest, where Violet and I go when we want to be alone together. Only tonight I am by myself. I have my oil lamp, and here I can sit and listen to the storm. I fear I am not truly alone, though. Something else is in here with me. I feel breath upon my neck, and although I want to believe it is the wind, I know it is not. I hear laughter, and it is not the sound of rain on the windows.

It is something else.

I fear I know what it is. That I know its name.

Rosemary.

I have come here to tell her to leave my sister alone. But now that I am here with her, I am afraid that she will take me too.

The entry ended there. Ava was afraid to turn the page. She didn't want to know what came next. With a shaking hand, she flipped to the next page before she could stop herself.

The page was empty.

She flipped some more pages. They were all blank. For whatever reason, Lily had stopped recording things in the diary. Frustrated, Ava snapped the book shut.

She thought about the final entry. She could practically feel the chill of the storm that Lily described, even though the house was currently very warm. She pictured the rooms lit only by gas lights or by candles, and how eerie that would be.

Mostly, she wondered about the place that Lily had mentioned. The angels' nest. What was that? Was it still there?

She thought about anything in the house that could be called a nest. Nothing fit that description. But then she remembered the little room at the top of the house. It was a small, square thing that seemed to perch atop the roof. You couldn't even see it from the ground. And Ava wasn't even sure how to get to it. She guessed through the attic. But she had been in the attic only once, briefly, when she and her mother had gone up there to see if there were any holes in the roof that needed to be repaired. There hadn't been, and so they'd come back down, and Ava hadn't thought about it again.

Until now.

Leaving her room and carrying the diary with her, she walked up the stairs to the third floor, then to the end of the hallway. There, a narrow set of stairs rose up to the attic door. Ava went up, opened the door, and stepped inside. She felt for the switch on the wall beside the door and flipped it.

The attic was lit by a string of bare bulbs that stretched from one end to the other. Only two were working, but it was enough to see by. Not that there was anything really to see. The attic was empty except for a few odds and ends: a broken wooden chair, a large empty frame from a painting, some old glass bottles.

Ava went deeper inside. Now she looked up toward the roof. And that's when she saw it. There, in the center, was a small square opening. It was covered from the other side with a piece of wood, and would have been easy to miss if she hadn't been looking for it.

She looked around for something to help her reach the opening. She wished she had a ladder. There was one downstairs, but she didn't want to attract Cassie's attention by going to get it. She needed another way.

Ava went into the farthest corner and discovered an old dresser there. It looked tall enough that if she stood on top, she might be able to reach the opening in the ceiling. She pushed on one side, and the heavy piece slid across the floor. She pushed again, angling it toward the center of the attic. It made a little noise, but she hoped Cassie wouldn't hear it.

When the dresser was below the opening near the roof, Ava climbed on top. Reaching up, she was able to press her fingertips against the square of wood. It moved. She pushed it some more, and slid it to the side. Now there was an opening. Weak sunlight came through, so Ava assumed that it led into the little room. But she still had to get up and inside.

She jumped up and grabbed on to the edge of the opening with both hands. Now she hung a little bit above the top of the dresser. Gritting her teeth, she slowly pulled herself up as if she was doing a pull-up. Her arms burned, but she was strong, and a moment later her head popped through the hole. Then she pushed herself the rest of the way in, ending up on her stomach.

She scooted into the room and rolled over. She was sure she had found the angels' nest.

The room was small, maybe six feet by six feet square. The perfect size for two sisters to hide in when they wanted to get away from everyone. There was a single window set into each wall, so you could look out in every direction. Ava could easily imagine Violet and Lily sitting up there together, reading their favorite books while the rain pattered gently on the roof, or napping in the warm sun as they dreamed about going on wonderful adventures.

Ava wanted to examine the room more closely, so she got up and went to one of the windows and rubbed away some of the dust that was covering the glass. As light flooded into the room and she got a better look, the pleasant mood vanished instantly.

Every inch of the walls and ceiling was covered with drawings of Rosemary, just like the one in Cassie's bedroom. Everywhere she looked, she saw the same black eyes, the same wild hair. The same mouth open in a scream.

10

Ava's first instinct was to get out of the angels' nest as quickly as she could. She even started to lower herself through the hole and back into the attic, so she wouldn't have to look at Rosemary's face anymore. The black eyes seemed to stare at her wherever she looked, and she wanted to get as far away from them as she could. But then she stopped herself. The diary had led her here for a reason, and if she wanted to help Cassie, she had to try to understand why.

Fighting the instinct to run, she got up and examined the drawings of Rosemary more closely. They appeared to have been drawn with a pencil. The lines were thick, suggesting that the person drawing them had scratched the pencil back and forth furiously, almost gouging the portraits into the wood. There were hundreds of them, all more or less identical but of different sizes, as if the artist had been determined to fill every available space. The open mouths screamed silently as the pairs of black eyes glared at Ava without blinking.

Ava walked to one of the windows and looked out. Through the dirt and grime, she could see the summerhouse. She went to the next window, which looked out over the backyard. The third window showed the front of the house. The fourth framed a view of the side yard, but that wasn't what Ava noticed when she looked at it. Instead, she found herself looking at another picture of Rosemary. This one was drawn in the dust that covered the glass, as if someone had stood there looking out and traced it with a finger. The lines of the drawing were clear, which meant it had been done recently.

Someone else had been in the angels' nest.

Ava wondered who else might have come up there. She couldn't imagine that either of her parents had. If they'd seen the room filled with creepy images of Rosemary, they would have said something about it. The only other person it might be was Cassie. And if Cassie had been there and not said anything to Ava about it, that was yet another secret they were keeping from each other.

Ava ran her own fingertip over the lines on the window. Had Cassie stood in that same spot, looking out and drawing the picture of Rosemary? Had she maybe even drawn all the other ones? Ava didn't think so. They looked older, like they'd been there a long time. But maybe Cassie *had* drawn them. Or at least some of them. She really hoped not. There was something very disturbing about all the pictures of the screaming girl.

Ava thought about Lily Blackthorn sitting in the room during the storm. What had she said about feeling someone's breath on her neck?

Just then, Ava felt something on *her* neck. She brushed it away with her hand, thinking it might be a spider. But there was nothing there. Then she felt it again, on the other side, as if someone was moving around behind her and leaning in to tickle her with a teasing puff of breath.

"Stop it!" she said, turning around. When she saw nobody there, she felt stupid.

But then she felt afraid. Thinking about what she'd read in Lily's diary, she wondered if maybe she wasn't alone after all. She wished she'd never come up to the little room. She wanted to get out of there, to be back down in the safety of her own bedroom.

Before she could leave, the piece of wood that covered the opening in the floor suddenly slid to the side all by itself. There was no way it could have been caused by wind or anything else natural. Something had moved it. Something invisible. Something that was now in the room with Ava.

Ava knelt down and tried to lift the piece of wood. It

wouldn't budge. It was as if it was glued to the floor or being held shut from the other side. But that was impossible. Ava gripped the edges of the covering until her fingernails were practically digging into the wood. She used all her strength, but it did nothing.

The room grew dark around her. Glancing at one of the windows, she saw that the world outside had turned dark. This didn't make any sense either. Seconds ago, there had been bright sunshine. Now it was practically as pitch-black as nighttime, even though it couldn't be much past noon. Then a loud rumble of thunder sounded, followed by a crack of lightning. Rain pelted against the window glass.

Just like the night Lily came up here, Ava thought.

The angels' nest rocked with the sound of the freak storm. It swirled around the little room, as if the wind and rain wanted to tear it to pieces. Ava's head filled with a roaring that quickly rose into a wailing scream. She covered her ears, trying to block it out, but it crept in between her fingers.

"Stop it!" she cried out. "Leave me alone!"

A flicker of lightning illuminated the room, showing the hundreds of Rosemarys with their mouths open. The screaming sound seemed to be coming from them, a chorus of shrieks that combined to form an unearthly howl. Ava closed her eyes, wishing she were anywhere else. She pounded on the hatch, the only way out.

"Help!" she heard herself call out. "Help! I'm trapped up here!"

From the other side came an answering pounding. A moment later, the hatch moved aside like it had never been stuck at all. Ava breathed a sigh of relief. She couldn't wait to get out of the room. Then she looked down and saw Cassie staring up at her, a scowl on her face.

"Why are you shouting?" she asked Ava.

"I was locked in," Ava explained. "And then the storm started and—"

"What storm?" said Cassie. "What are you talking about?"

"The storm," Ava repeated. "Don't you hear the wind and the thunder? The rain?"

Cassie shook her head. "It's sunny out," she said. "Look."

Ava turned and looked at one of the windows. Sure enough, even through the streaks of dirt she could see that it was bright and clear outside. There was no storm. The glass wasn't even wet. And the howling that had filled the angels' nest had stopped too.

"I guess I imagined it," she said.

"You must have some imagination," said Cassie. "I could hear you all the way in my room. You sounded like you were being murdered."

"I . . . don't know what happened," Ava said, unable to explain to her sister what she'd experienced. "It was all so real."

"What are you doing up there anyway?" asked Cassie. "What is this? And how did you even find it?"

"Oh," Ava said, thinking quickly. She didn't want to tell Cassie about the diary. "I was just poking around in the attic and noticed the hatch. I wondered what it led to."

"Well, now you know," Cassie said. "Good thing I was here to hear you. You might have been stuck up there forever."

Ava shuddered at the thought of being stuck in the little room with all the drawings of Rosemary. She glanced up at the wall. When she did, she heard herself gasp. "They're gone," she said.

"What's gone?" said Cassie.

"The drawings," Ava said, getting to her feet. She turned around. All the walls were bare. Where the images of Rosemary had been, there was just faded wallpaper. "But that's impossible. They were here. I saw them."

"Drawings?" Cassie said. "Drawings of what?"

"Of Rose . . ." Ava started to tell her, then stopped. "Roses," she lied, running her fingers over the blank walls. "Drawings of roses. The walls were covered in them."

Cassie looked at the walls. "You know what I think?" she said.

"What?" Ava asked. She was looking at the window where the drawing of Rosemary had appeared on the dusty glass. It too was gone.

"I think you were dreaming," Cassie said. "I think you came up here, sat down in the sun, and fell asleep. You probably dreamed about roses because we've been working in the garden so much. Then you dreamed there was a storm, scared yourself, and woke up thinking it was real."

Ava knew that this wasn't what had happened. She *had* seen the drawings of Rosemary. She *had* heard a storm. And she had *not* been dreaming. *Then how do you explain that the drawings aren't here now?* she asked herself.

That question, she couldn't answer.

"Anyway, get out of there," Cassie said. "There could be bats or something."

"Yeah," Ava agreed, anxious to be away from the room.

She slipped her legs through the hole and let herself fall through, landing on the dresser next to Cassie. The two of them got down. Ava looked back up at the still-open hatch. She knew there were no bats in the angels' nest. But there was *something* in there.

Something much, much worse.

11

"I can't believe it. The roses are coming back!"

Ava turned from her spot in the yard to see who had spoken. Two heavyset men stood in the driveway. One was white, with short silver hair and a bushy beard the same color. The other was Black, and he also had a beard, although his head was smooth as an egg. Both men were wearing jeans and plaid shirts—one blue and yellow and the other purple and red—and both had leather suspenders holding up their pants. They reminded Ava of two friendly bears, and she liked them immediately.

"Hi," said the bald man, waving to her and her mom. "I'm Ed."

"And I'm Colin," said the silver-haired man. "We brought you a pie."

"Peach," Ed added as they walked closer, and Ed held out a red dish.

"Why, thank you," said Ava's mother. "That's so kind of you. I'm Janet Chapel, by the way. And this is my daughter Ava."

"We know," Colin said. "Your husband is Brad and your other daughter is Cassie." When Ava's mother looked surprised, he added, "Rhoda—the Realtor who sold you the house—told us."

"The woman cannot keep a secret," Ed said, and both men laughed.

"Brad and Cassie are running some errands in town," Ava's mother said. "Ava and I came out to look at the roses and discovered new leaves on them."

The two men walked over to one of the rosebushes and

inspected it. "I never thought they'd grow again," Colin said. "After Lily died, so did they. Just withered up overnight. It was the strangest thing. It was like they were grieving for her."

"You knew Lily?" Ava asked.

Colin nodded. "Sorry," he said. "I should have told you earlier. We're your neighbors. Two down, on the other side of the street."

"The blue Victorian house with the huge porch?" Ava's mother said. "It's so beautiful."

"Thank you," Ed said. "We've done a lot to it since we moved in." He looked at Colin. "How many years ago now?"

"Twenty-seven," Colin answered. "You had hair and I had just started teaching at the college."

"What do you teach?" Ava's mother asked.

"American history," said Colin. Then he looked at Ava. "And to answer your question, we did indeed know Lily Blackthorn. She was already quite old when we moved in. Over ninety, I think. She barely ever saw anyone. But this one"—he pointed at Ed—"made her one of his pies and left it on her doorstep with a note. Three days later, she called and invited us for tea. After that, we saw her fairly regularly."

"It was blueberry," Ed said thoughtfully. "We're so happy that you bought the house. It's been empty for far too long. It needed people in it."

"What was Lily like?" Ava asked.

Ed and Colin exchanged a look. "Sad," Colin said.

"More like haunted," said Ed.

"That's it," Colin agreed. "Haunted. I can't think of a better word to describe her."

"Haunted?" said Ava, a chill running over her skin as she thought about what people said about their house. "What do you mean?"

Ed sighed. "Lily was a very lonely person," he said. "After her sister died, she felt all alone."

"Violet," Ava said.

"That's right," said Ed. "She died in 1916 from scarlet

fever. It affected lots of people around that time. Your house belonged to their aunt Daisy. The girls were sent here because their parents thought they would be safer in the country than in the crowded city where they lived. Unfortunately, that wasn't true, at least not for Violet. Lily didn't get sick, which is a miracle given that they spent all of their time together."

"How terrible for her, to lose her sister," Ava's mother said, putting her arm around Ava.

"Not just her sister," Colin said. "Her twin. And they were only twelve."

"The same age as me and Cassie," Ava said. "So, if this was their aunt's house, how did Lily end up living here?"

"That's a whole other story," said Ed. "Daisy Blackthorn never married. Neither did Lily. After that terrible summer, she returned home to her parents. But when she was eighteen, she moved back here to be her aunt's companion. She never left. When Daisy died, Lily inherited the house."

"And she lived here all alone?" said Ava.

"Well, that depends who you ask," said Colin. "There were what she and Daisy called 'the friends.' But they weren't people. At least not living ones."

Ava felt a prickle of fear tickle her neck. "You mean ghosts?" she said.

"Daisy and Lily called them spirits," Colin explained. "Daisy was very interested in Spiritualism. Communicating with the dead through mediums. She apparently thought she *was* a medium. She used to hold séances here."

Ava wanted to tell them about the cassette tape they'd found in the wall. But she didn't want to remind her mother about it, as she had no idea if Cassie had put it back or still had it hidden somewhere.

"According to Lily, there were often spirits in the house," Colin continued. "Lily believed that Violet's spirit sometimes visited them as well. It's one of the reasons she stayed here, even when the money she inherited ran out and she couldn't afford to maintain it. It's why the house was in the shape it was when she died."

"We tried to help as much as we could," Ed added. "I have an antiques store in town. Whenever we could tell Lily needed money, I would offer to buy one of the pieces in the house. We'd move it into storage, then bring it back a few months later. By then she was having a hard time remembering things, so she never noticed."

"That was kind of you," Ava's mother said. "What a sad thing for her to believe about her sister. And how awful to be in this big old house all by herself."

"We still have a number of things from the house," Ed said. "Some of the artwork. A few pieces of furniture. You're welcome to have them if you like."

"I found some of Violet and Lily's books, I think," Ava said. "In the summerhouse."

"Then you might be interested in this box of photos and journals I have," Ed told her. "Lots of pictures of Lily and Violet. And I think a couple of diaries."

"I'd *love* to see those!" Ava said.

"They're over at the house," said Ed. "If it's all right

with your mom, you can come over and take a look."

"Now?" Ava said. She turned to her mother. "Is it okay?"

"Ed and Colin might be busy, honey."

"I'm not," said Ed. "And I bet Colin would love to show you his roses."

"Absolutely," said Colin. "Ed gets tired of hearing me talk about them. It will be nice to have a new person to bore to tears."

"All right, then," Ava's mother said. "Maybe I'll get some ideas about what to do with our roses. I don't even know where to start."

As Colin started talking animatedly about roses, they all walked out of the yard.

"Your mother has no idea what she's gotten herself into," Ed whispered to Ava as they walked ahead of Colin and Ava's mom. "He could talk about roses all day."

Ava laughed. "If he can help get the roses looking like they used to, she'll be thrilled. Did they really all die overnight?"

Ed nodded. "It was so odd. I can't explain it. It's like when Lily died, they couldn't live anymore. And they never grew again. Not until now."

Ava suddenly wanted to tell him about all the peculiar things that were going on in the house, and with Cassie. She'd been holding it all inside, wishing she had some-one she could talk to about it, and Ed seemed like he would listen to her and not think she was making it all up or imagining things. But she couldn't quite do it. Instead, she said, "Do you think Daisy and Lily really were able to talk to dead people?"

Ed didn't answer for a long moment, and Ava wondered if maybe she'd said something wrong. Then he said, "I know *Lily* believed that they did. I think that's what mattered. It helped her feel like she hadn't completely lost her sister."

They reached the house where Ed and Colin lived. As Colin took Ava's mother to look at the rose garden, Ed walked up the steps and opened the front door. They stepped inside, and Ed led Ava into the living room.

"Have a seat," he said. "I'll be right back."

Ava sat down on a couch that looked like an antique but was surprisingly comfortable. The entire room was filled with beautiful pieces of furniture, and the walls were covered with all kinds of paintings, some that looked really old and others that were modern. But they all worked together somehow. She wondered if Blackthorn House would look as good when they were done fixing it up.

"Here we are," Ed said, returning to the room carrying a cardboard box. He set it down on the coffee table in front of the couch, then took a seat beside Ava.

Opening the box, he removed a large envelope. "I think these are the most interesting," he said as he slid a stack of photos out and handed them to Ava. "Most of these are photos of Lily and Violet. But some are, well, more unusual."

"Unusual how?" asked Ava.

"You'll see," Ed said mysteriously.

Ava looked at the photograph on top. Lily and Violet stood among the roses in the courtyard. They were dressed in identical white dresses, with their long hair in two braids.

"Who took this?" Ava asked. "Daisy?"

"Yes," said Ed. "She was very interested in photography, mainly because she wanted to capture images of spirits."

"And did she?"

"Keep going," Ed urged. "See for yourself."

Curious, Ava flipped through the stack of photos more quickly. After a dozen or so ordinary ones, she came to one that was different. It showed Lily and Violet seated at a table. Their hands were placed on the tabletop, their fingers touching. In the middle of the image, seeming to hover in the air about six inches over their hands, was what looked like a small ball of light.

"What is that?" Ava asked, looking more closely.

"Supposedly, a spirit," said Ed. "Daisy thought that Lily and Violet were born mediums. According to Lily, she often made them sit and try to contact the dead while she took photos of the manifestations."

Ava looked at the next photo, which was similar to the first except that Lily and Violet were wearing different dresses and there were three balls of light over the table.

"Spirit photography was very popular at that time," Ed told Ava. "Mostly of it was faked. But Lily swore her aunt never did anything more than take pictures of what actually happened during those sessions."

Ava flipped to the next photo. This time, she let out a little gasp of surprise.

"That's the one," Ed said. "Creepy, isn't it?"

Ava could only nod. Once again, Lily and Violet were seated with their hands touching. But this time, a ghostly figure appeared to be standing between the two of them. It was another girl. She was very faint, the features of her face blurred as if she were made of white smoke. Her long hair floated all around her head. And her mouth was open in a scream. On either side of her, Lily and Violet looked up at her, their eyes wide with fright.

"Rosemary," Ava heard herself say.

"How did you know that's what they called her?" Ed asked, sounding surprised.

"Oh, um, we found a picture of her," Ava said, unable to take her eyes away from the photograph. "A drawing, I mean. Not a photo. She looked a lot like this."

"That's what Lily called her too," Ed said. "But she wouldn't talk about her, so we have no idea who she might have been."

Ava couldn't stop staring at the photo of the three girls. Her thoughts were all jumbled together as she tried to make connections between the things she'd discovered. She still had no idea what it all meant. But one thing was clear.

Rosemary was real.

12

"It's a twister! It's a twister!"

Steph Giamotta turned and looked in Ava's direction. "It's a twister!" she shouted again.

Ava, who had been thinking about other things, suddenly realized that she'd missed her cue. Now she pulled hard on the rope in her hand. Too hard. At the other side of the stage, the huge tornado that Mr. Bremen, the art teacher, had fashioned out of chicken wire and strips of gauzy gray fabric lurched out of the wings and headed for the students playing Aunt Em, Uncle Henry, and the three farmhands—Hunk, Zeke, and Hickory. One of those students was Cassie, who had the dual role of Hunk and the Scarecrow.

The tornado swirled wildly, its narrow tail whipping around as Ava tried to slow it down. But it was moving too quickly. A moment later it crashed into the group of actors. Steph (who was Zeke/the Cowardly Lion) and Liam Winesap (Uncle Henry) went down, while the other three grabbed at the out-of-control twister and attempted to stop it. It continued to twirl, and they all got tangled up in it and in one another's arms and legs.

Mr. Bremen ran over to Ava and grabbed the rope from her hands.

"Sorry," Ava apologized.

The students watching from the floor in front of the stage howled with laughter as the ones onstage worked themselves free from the chicken-wire tornado or picked themselves up.

"I'm sorry," Ava said again.

"It's okay," Mr. Bremen assured her. "At least we know the thing works!"

"Is everyone all right?" asked Mr. Chowdry, coming up onstage.

All the actors said that they were fine. This made Ava feel a little bit better. She looked at Cassie, hoping her sister would flash her a reassuring smile, but Cassie didn't even give her a glance.

Ava hadn't yet showed Cassie the photos she'd gotten from Ed the day before. Well, she hadn't showed her *all* of them. She'd shared the more ordinary ones. But she'd kept the one of Rosemary to herself.

Cassie hadn't seemed particularly interested. She'd looked at the photographs briefly, handed them back, then gone to her room, supposedly to learn her lines. But when Ava had stopped outside her door later on, she'd heard Cassie whispering to someone. And she had a pretty good idea who that someone was.

Ever since Ed had told her how Lily believed that Violet's

spirit visited her in the house, Ava had been thinking about it. She didn't know if she believed in ghosts or spirits or anything like that. But in the past couple of weeks, she'd seen and experienced things that were definitely *not* normal. Maybe some of it could be explained by her imagination. But not all of it. Something was definitely going on in Blackthorn House. And whoever—or whatever—Rosemary was, she was at the center of it.

The worst part was that she was dragging Cassie into it. Again, Ava wasn't sure how, or why, but she was pretty certain that Rosemary was focusing all her attention on Cassie. But for what reason? Ava just didn't know enough to be able to come up with an explanation. And every time she even mentioned Rosemary to her sister, Cassie grew more distant. It was as if Rosemary was this invisible wall between them, and she was getting stronger every day.

"Okay," Mr. Chowdry called out. "Let's try this again. Sam, is everything working right?"

Mr. Bremen gave Mr. Chowdry a thumbs-up sign. Then

he handed the rope to Ava. "Everything looks good," he said. "I adjusted the counterweight. Pull it firmly but slowly and the tornado will slide along the rail behind the lights and spin around on its own. Just to be on the safe side, though, let's get you a partner."

He looked around and waved to someone standing on the other side of the stage. "Beth-Ann!" he called out as Ava groaned.

Beth-Ann frowned as she came over. Like the other actors who weren't in the scene, she was supposed to be a stagehand. But Ava had never seen her do anything other than talk with her friends while everyone else did the actual work.

"I want you to stand here with Ava," Mr. Bremen told her. "If anything goes wrong with the tornado, you help her out."

"You mean stop her from killing anyone," Beth-Ann said, laughing as if this was the funniest joke anyone had ever told. "She practically took their heads off."

"I didn't do anything," Ava muttered.

"Just stand here and be ready," said Mr. Bremen. "I'm sure it will be fine."

Mr. Bremen left. Beth-Ann sighed and leaned against the wall. "This is so boring," she complained. "I mean, at least I'm not a flying monkey and a tornado wrangler, but still."

Ava ignored her. Mr. Chowdry was giving some direction to the actors. She wished he would finish so they could start again. Mr. Chowdry said something to Cassie, who laughed.

"It must be tough having your sister get a better part than you did," Beth-Ann said.

"She got a better part than you did too," Ava reminded her.

"You know what I think?" Beth-Ann said. She didn't wait for Ava to reply. "I think you made that prop go crazy because you *wanted* Cassie to get hurt. Then you could have her part."

"What?" Ava said, turning and looking at the other girl. "First of all, I would never hurt my sister. Second, why would I get her part if she got hurt?"

Beth-Ann grinned. "That's true," she said. "It's not like you can sing. But still, if she wasn't in the show, you'd get more attention."

"That's the dumbest thing I've—"

"Okay!" Mr. Chowdry called out. "We're going to try the scene again. Stagehands, are you ready?"

Ava turned away from Beth-Ann. "Ready!" she called out.

Mr. Chowdry left the stage and returned to his seat in what would be the front row of the audience once all the chairs were set up for the actual performances. "Action!" he called out.

Steph pointed toward the right side of the stage. "It's a twister!" she said. "It's a twister!"

Ava tugged on the rope.

Nothing happened.

She felt herself start to panic. She tugged again.

This time, the wire-and-cloth tornado emerged from the shadows of the stage. Ava felt herself breathe more easily. But then she looked more closely. Something was odd about the fake twister. Inside the funnel of chicken wire, something swirled. It was like a dark mist or cloud. While the tornado inched across the stage, the darkness appeared to thicken. As Ava stared, the darkness seemed to take the form of a girl floating inside the tornado.

"Do you see that?" Ava asked Beth-Ann.

"See what?" Beth-Ann said. "The stupid twister? Of course I see it."

"No," Ava said. "Inside of it."

The tornado was designed so that it turned as it moved. The pieces of cloth fluttered, hiding the thing inside it. But whenever an area of wire appeared with nothing covering it, the ghostly figure could be seen. It looked exactly like the photograph of Rosemary.

"There!" Ava said, pointing. "Do you see it now?"

Beth-Ann gasped.

"You do, don't you?" Ava said.

"What *is* that?" said Beth-Ann. "Some kind of special effect?"

"It's Rosemary," Ava whispered.

"Who?" Beth-Ann asked. "There's nobody named Rosemary in our school."

Before Ava could say anything else, the ghostly form raised its hands. A chilly wind blew across the stage, and the tornado started to spin faster. The actors stepped away from the prop twister and looked at it. Then they looked at Ava.

"It's not me!" Ava said.

The tornado turned faster. Ava could feel the rope tense, as if someone was trying to tug it out of her hands. As the twister turned more and more quickly, she caught only tiny glimpses of the apparition hiding inside it.

The wind picked up, swirling around the stage. The curtains on either side fluttered. Then pages of the script that were lying on the floor lifted up and began to twirl like leaves. So did other small items.

Beth-Ann let out a sharp gasp. "It's a real . . ." she said.

"A real what?" Ava said.

For a moment, she thought Beth-Ann was going to admit that she'd seen a ghost. Instead, Beth-Ann said, "A real tornado. It's a real tornado."

"Everybody off the stage!" Mr. Chowdry yelled as the twister bucked and lurched against the rope.

Ava's hands burned from trying to keep the twister under control. Then it was yanked away from her. She cried out in pain and looked at her palms, where two red welts appeared. She was distracted from the injury by the sound of people crying out in fear. When she looked up, she saw the tornado spinning wildly as the cast members scrambled to get away from it. But wherever they moved, the twister moved too, blocking their escape. Papers pelted them, and they put their hands up to protect themselves.

Only Cassie seemed calm. She stood in the middle of the stage, staring into the dark, swirling center of the storm and smiling. Seeing her, Ava felt chilled to the bone. It was like Cassie was looking at a friend.

"What's she doing?" Beth-Ann said. "She looks *happy*."

"Cassie!" Ava shouted.

Cassie didn't turn around.

Ava ran onto the stage. Aisha joined her, and the two of them dashed over to where Cassie stood, transfixed. Ava grabbed her sister.

"Make her stop!" Ava said, shaking Cassie. "She's going to hurt someone!"

Cassie didn't respond. It was as if she were frozen. Her unblinking eyes stared at the spinning tornado. Ava shook her again. Cassie swayed like a tree in a storm.

"Cassie!" Aisha shouted, but got no response. She looked at Ava, her face filled with fear. "What's wrong with her?"

Ava turned her attention to the twister. She approached it.

"Whatever you're doing, stop," she shouted.

The wind blew harder. A piece of balled-up paper hit Ava in the side of the face.

"Rosemary!" Ava shouted. "I know you're doing this. Stop it!"

The tornado spun around and around. Through the gaps in the cloth, Ava saw the ghostly image of a girl staring back at her. But Ava knew Rosemary wasn't going to stop. She had to do something else.

Reaching out, she grabbed at the chicken wire that formed the body of the twister. Her fingers found holes in it and she gripped it tightly. But now it started to drag her as it turned. Her feet slipped on the polished wood floor as she fought to try to control the tornado. Inside, Rosemary glared out at her with pale, ghostly eyes.

"You. Have. To. Stop." Ava choked the words out as she was twirled around.

She could feel Rosemary trying to make the twister

move even more quickly. But Ava hung on, and her weight started to pull the tornado down. She let herself go limp, so that she was deadweight on the chicken wire. She felt herself slipping, but she pushed her fingers deeper into the wire, feeling it cut into her skin.

The chicken wire gave way. The twister fell apart, and Ava tumbled to the floor. She rolled over, becoming entangled in the cloth and wire. Everything that had been floating in the air fell to the floor around her. When she looked over at Cassie, she saw her sister shaking her head as Aisha put her arm around Cassie's shoulders. Cassie looked as if she had just woken up from a dream.

"Cassie?" Ava called out. "Are you okay?"

Cassie turned and looked at Ava. "What did you do?" she said to her sister.

"Yeah," said JJ Darby, who was playing the Tin Man and who now stood looking down at Ava. "What did you do? That thing went crazy."

"I stopped it," Ava said as she disentangled herself from the remnants of the tornado.

"You destroyed it," said Hannah Sykes, who was playing Aunt Em.

Now everyone was standing around Ava in a circle, looking at her with peculiar expressions on their faces. Only Mr. Chowdry reached down and helped Ava get up. But even he seemed confused.

"I had to do it," Ava said. "It was the only way to stop her."

"Stop who?" asked Mr. Bremen, eyeing the broken prop with a sad expression.

Ava looked at Cassie, but her sister wouldn't meet her gaze. Even Aisha was looking at her with an expression she couldn't read. Did she think Ava was responsible too?

"It," Ava said. "I had to stop it. The twister."

"Well, you did that," said Steph.

Ava walked over to Cassie. "Did you see her?" she

asked in a low voice so that no one else would hear her.

"See who?" Cassie replied.

"Rosemary," Ava said. "She was inside the tornado. This is all her fault."

Cassie frowned. "That's insane," she said coldly.

Ava looked around for Beth-Ann, who was still standing to the side of the stage. She took Cassie by the arm and dragged her over to Beth-Ann. "You saw her," she said to Beth-Ann. "The girl. Tell her."

For a moment, Beth-Ann looked like she might confirm Ava's story. She opened her mouth. Then she closed it. "I don't know what you're talking about," she said. "I didn't see any girl. Unless you mean you. I saw you run out there and destroy our best set piece."

"You did too see her!" Ava said. "You know you did."

Beth-Ann gave Cassie a pitying look. "I'm sorry your sister is jealous of you," she said.

Ava felt her face flush. She was so angry she didn't know what to do. Her whole body was shaking. She stormed off, stomping down the stage stairs and then running out of the auditorium.

As she raced down the hallway toward the front doors, she was sure she heard the sound of laughter following her.

13

"Is someone going to tell me why you're all being weird?" Gwen asked.

She was sitting in the back seat of Aisha's mother's car, sandwiched between Cassie and Ava. Aisha was in the front passenger seat. It was Mrs. Bashir's turn to pick everyone up from their practices and take them out for pizza.

When nobody answered her, Gwen looked at Ava, then at Cassie. "Okay, then," she said when neither of them acknowledged her. "I guess I'll just have to tell you *every single thing* we did at soccer practice. First, we started with dribbling skills. Coach Calfstock had us start at one end of the field and run down, then back, in pairs. I ran with Eloise Molton and beat her by three whole seconds. So then—"

"Okay!" Aisha said. "We're all just a little freaked out because there was an—incident—at play practice."

"That's better," Gwen said happily. "What kind of incident?"

Again, nobody spoke up. Finally, Aisha said, "It wasn't that big a deal. The fake tornado kind of went wild. It spun around and knocked some people down. That's all."

"What?" Mrs. Bashir said, sounding concerned. "Is everyone okay?"

"Everyone is fine," Aisha assured her.

"You're not *acting* fine," said Gwen. "You sure nothing else happened?"

"Positive," Aisha said firmly.

Gwen didn't say anything in response, and she stayed quiet until they got to the pizza restaurant, sat down, and Mrs. Bashir left the four of them alone while she went to look at yarn at the shop next door.

"You still gonna pretend nothing happened?" Gwen said as the other three stared at their menus.

"Why don't you tell us some more about what a good dribbler you are," Aisha suggested.

"Uh-uh," said Gwen. "Now I *know* something happened." She looked from Cassie to Ava. "How come you two aren't saying anything?"

"Aisha already told you, we had issues with the tornado prop," Ava said. She wished Gwen would drop the subject. All she wanted was to eat her pizza and go home.

Gwen didn't. "If everyone is okay, why are you all acting like something else happened? Something big."

"I have to use the restroom," Cassie announced, and got up.

As she walked away, Ava made a decision. "I have to tell you both something," she said, setting her menu down. "You remember all the weird stuff about the séance?"

"Sure," Gwen said as Aisha nodded.

"And you remember that person Lily Blackthorn talked about? Rosemary?"

"Yeah," said Gwen. "What's that got to do with a fake tornado and everybody acting like there's some big secret?"

"I think Rosemary caused the accident," Ava said. "I think she's real."

"Real?" Aisha said.

"As in a real ghost?" Gwen added.

"Well, I don't know if she's a ghost," Ava said. "I don't know what she is. But I'm pretty sure she's real. And there's more."

"More?" said Aisha. "Like a ghost isn't bad enough."

"I think she's doing something to Cassie."

"What kind of something?" asked Gwen.

"I don't know, exactly," Ava answered. "But Cassie has been acting weird. And I've found out some stuff about what happened the summer that Lily and Violet lived in our house and Violet died. I think Rosemary was involved with that too."

"You mean we've got ourselves a *killer* ghost?" said Gwen. "That's a problem."

"Like I said, I don't know what she is," Ava said. "But yeah, we've got a problem. And I don't know what to do about it."

"And this ghost—Rosemary—caused the accident with the tornado?" said Aisha.

"You don't believe me," Ava said.

Aisha hesitated. "I believe you *think* you saw something," she said.

Ava's stomach sank. "You're the one who told me about there being a ghost in our house in the first place," she said angrily. "Now that I'm telling you there is one, you think I'm lying?"

"I don't think you're lying," said Aisha. "I just think maybe you've been thinking about those stories so much that you're using them as a reason for things."

"She was inside the tornado," said Ava. "Rosemary. I saw her. So did Beth-Ann, although then she pretended that she didn't."

"Beth-Ann got to see a ghost, and I didn't?" Gwen said. "That's so not fair."

"And now everybody thinks I'm the one who did everything," Ava continued. She gave Aisha a look. "Including my friends, apparently."

"Aisha didn't say that," Gwen said. "Not exactly."

"Hey!" Aisha exclaimed. "I didn't say I blame Ava for anything. I'm just not sure I think it's a ghost, is all."

Gwen crossed her arms and looked at Aisha. "Ava's our friend," she said. "And friends stick together." Then she looked at Ava. "Even when they might be dragging us into something like chasing a ghost that might or might not be real."

"All right," Aisha said after a moment. She sounded like she did when she had an idea. "If we're going to do this, we need a plan. And the first step in every plan is to get information. Ava, you said you found some stuff, right?"

Ava nodded. "I have Lily's journal," she said. "And some photos I got from our neighbor. There might also be some more stuff in that box. I'll look tonight."

"That's a good start," said Aisha. "I think we should try to find out if Rosemary was a real person. Maybe there are some records of her somewhere. I'll look into that."

"Everybody's getting an assignment," Gwen remarked. "What's mine?"

"You find out everything you can about ghosts," said Aisha. "See if there's anything about them hurting people, or making bad things happen."

"I can do that," Gwen said confidently.

"But we can't let Cassie know we're doing any of this," Ava warned them. "I know this will sound weird, but I think if she knows, then Rosemary will know."

"That doesn't sound any weirder than anything else you've said," Gwen told her. "Anyway, here comes Cassie now. Everyone act normal."

"I think I'm going to try the pineapple and red pepper pizza," Aisha said. "What's everyone else getting?"

"Probably the BBQ chicken one," Gwen said. "With extra hot sauce."

"The funguspalooza with five kinds of mushrooms sounds great," said Ava as her sister sat down. "Cassie, are you getting the garlic, tomato, and feta cheese like last time? You really liked that."

"No," Cassie said sharply. "I want to try one with bacon and sausage. Maybe pepperoni too."

"But you don't eat meat," said Ava, shocked.

Cassie shrugged. "I guess I do now," she said.

Ava exchanged glances with Gwen and Aisha. This was one more strange thing to add to the list. But she wasn't about to make Cassie angry, especially after what had happened during rehearsal, so she let it go. Instead, when their food came, she changed the subject to schoolwork, and they talked about their classes. At least, she and Gwen and Aisha did. Cassie barely said anything. She was too busy eating her pizza, which she devoured as if she were starving. Usually, she only ate half and took the rest home. But she wolfed down every piece, then looked like she wished there were more.

Ava was relieved when Mrs. Bashir came back with two bags full of yarn and they headed home. When they got out in front of Blackthorn House, she thanked Aisha's mother while Cassie walked up to the porch without even saying goodbye.

"We'll talk tomorrow," Ava told Gwen and Aisha, trying to sound like everything was fine so Mrs. Bashir wouldn't notice the tension. "And thanks for helping me with my, uh, homework."

When she got inside, Cassie had already disappeared upstairs.

"How did practice go?" Ava's dad asked. He was doing something with the kitchen sink, and there were parts all over the counter.

"Okay," Ava said. She didn't think he needed to be filled in on all the details.

"Did you have fun at dinner?" her father continued. "Cassie ran upstairs so fast I didn't get a chance to ask her."

"Yeah," Ava said. "It was great. But I've got a ton of homework to do."

"Okay," said her dad, picking up a wrench and disappearing under the sink. "Have fun."

Upstairs, Ava glanced at Cassie's bedroom door, which was shut, and went to her room. She retrieved the box Ed had given her from her closet and sat down on the floor with it. She took out the photos and looked through them again. When she came to the one that showed Rosemary hovering between Lily and Violet, she examined it for a long time. The girl—the *thing*—she'd seen inside the twister definitely looked the same. Ava shuddered, remembering how the blank eyes had stared out at her. She turned the photo over and set the stack of pictures aside.

Underneath the photos were various things, including a lot of old newspaper articles about the fever epidemic that had killed so many people in 1916. Ava didn't spend too long looking at these. She was more interested in something that fell out of one of the folded-up newspapers. It was a stack of letters. Each one was addressed to Mrs. Henry Blackthorn at 39 Morningwood Lane in Philadelphia, Pennsylvania.

Oddly, none of the letters had been opened. Each one remained sealed, as if they had never been mailed, or Mrs. Henry Blackthorn had never received them. Ava took the letter on top of the pile, turned it over, and pulled at the corner of the back flap. It opened a little bit, and she was able to slide her fingertip underneath and unseal it. She took out a single sheet of paper, folded in thirds, and unfolded it.

She recognized the handwriting from Lily's diary. It was exactly the same. The ink, sealed inside the envelope for more than a hundred years, was only slightly faded.

Dearest Mother,

I am sorry to write to you with unpleasant news, but I do not know what else to do. As you know, Violet is unwell. But I fear there is something more wrong with her than just the fever. I do not know how to put this into words that will make sense, but I feel that she is being tormented by something else. Something for which I do not have a name.

"What are you doing?"

Ava, startled, looked up. Cassie was standing in the doorway. But she looked different. It took Ava a moment to realize what it was. Then she realized that Cassie had changed how she wore her hair. It no longer fell loosely around her shoulders. Instead, she had worked it into two long braids. She looked very old-fashioned. *She looks like Violet*, Ava thought.

"What are you doing?" Cassie said again.

"Oh," Ava said. "Nothing. Just looking at some stuff."

She quickly folded the letter and stuffed it back into the envelope. Then she gathered up the other letters and put them underneath one of the newspapers.

"Those don't belong to you," Cassie said. "Give them to me." She held out her hand.

Ava felt herself grow angry. "No," she said. "They don't belong to you either. They're letters Lily Blackthorn wrote to her mother. And I'm going to read them. If you want to read them after that, you can. But I'm reading them first."

Cassie frowned. "You're going to be sorry," she said.

"Is that you saying that?" Ava asked her. "Or Rosemary?"

Cassie snorted. "You don't know what you're talking about," she said. She turned around and walked into the hall.

Ava got up and shut her door. Then she retrieved the bundle of letters. "You're right," she said. "I don't know what I'm talking about. But maybe these will help me figure it out."

14

"Is Cassie already out front waiting for the bus?" Ava asked.

It was the next morning, and she was running late because she'd stayed up until after one o'clock reading the letters from Lily Blackthorn to her and Violet's mother. Discovering what was in them had made her even more concerned about what was going on with Cassie, and she wanted to talk to Aisha and Gwen about it. She didn't know how she could do that, though, given that Cassie was around almost every period.

"No," her mother said, handing her a piece of toast. "Cassie isn't feeling well, so she's staying home."

"What's wrong with her?" Ava asked as she spread peanut butter on the toast.

"She's just running a fever," her mother said. "I don't think it's anything serious, but I said she should stay home today. Tell your teachers, okay?"

Ava nodded. But she wasn't thinking about their teachers. She was thinking about the box of letters that was sitting in her closet. If Cassie was home, she could—and would—go looking for them to see what was in them. Ava didn't want that to happen.

"I'll be right back," she said, setting the toast down and heading for the stairs. "I forgot my math book."

She went into her closet and took out the stack of letters. She left everything else there, as Cassie had already seen the photographs and nothing else in the box was very important. The letters were different. Those, Ava took back downstairs and slipped into her backpack. She was zipping it closed when her father walked through the front door.

"Have you seen the roses?" he asked.

"No," Ava's mother said. "Why?"

"They're everywhere," said Ava's father. "And they're blooming."

Ava's mother headed outside. Ava followed. When she reached the front porch, she stopped and stared.

"Wow," her mother said. "I can't believe all this happened since yesterday."

The rosebushes had nearly doubled in size. Some of them had started to creep up the sides of the summerhouse. And all of them were covered with roses that were such a deep red color that they almost appeared to be black. They were beautiful. But there was also something eerie about them.

"That scent is something else," Ava's father said, sniffing the air. "I don't even know how to describe it."

Ava took a deep breath. The perfume of the Blackthorn roses worked its way into her head. It made Ava think of a shady forest, and rain, and a night sky filled with stars. She couldn't say why, but those were the images that came to her. She didn't even know how to describe the scent itself, which was sweet and dark and somehow a little bit sad.

"Wait until Colin sees this," Ava's mother said. She sounded excited. "And we need to get photographs to put up on the website."

As Ava's father went inside to get his camera, the school bus pulled up in front of the house and the driver gave a little honk to let Ava know she was there. Ava waved to her mother and walked to the bus, where she took her usual seat by Gwen.

"Where's Cassie?" Gwen asked.

"Sick," said Ava. "She has a fever."

"Just like Violet," Gwen remarked.

"Hopefully not exactly like," said Ava. "But yeah, I thought of that too. And I'm glad she's not here, because now we can talk about what I found in the letters."

"I found out some stuff too," Gwen informed her. "Let's wait for Aisha to get on, though, so we don't have to go through it twice."

Although it was only about ten minutes before they got to Aisha's house, it felt like forever. Ava was dying to talk about what was in the letters, and Gwen was equally excited to reveal the results of her research. When Aisha got on and sat down, they both started talking at once.

"Lily tried to tell their mother that—" Ava began.

"Ghosts don't usually—" Gwen said at the same time.

They both paused and Aisha jumped in. "I couldn't find a single person named Rosemary in Ebenezer. Ever. The historical society has records online going back to when the town was founded, and there's nobody with that name. A lot of Roses, and a lot of Marys, but no Rosemarys. That doesn't mean she *wasn't* a real person. She could have lived in Blackthorn House, or visited, or died somewhere else and come here just to haunt your house. Or maybe that wasn't her real name. But I couldn't find out anything about her. Sorry." She sounded disappointed.

"That's okay," Ava reassured her. "Good work finding those records."

"Okay, let me tell you about ghosts," Gwen said, unable to keep quiet a second longer. "This might help."

Ava, who was anxious to tell them her own news, laughed. "All right," she said. "What did you find out?"

"Well, it's pretty obvious that ghosts are the spirits of people who have died," Gwen said. "I mean, they don't just show up out of nowhere, right? They had to be living people first. And they usually hang around the place where the person died. If Rosemary was a real girl who died in Blackthorn House, it would make sense that she was still there."

"But what if she *wasn't* a real person?" Aisha said.

"Then she's probably not a ghost," said Gwen. "She's something else."

"Like what?" asked Ava.

"There are things that *act* like ghosts but aren't," said Gwen. "Like poltergeists. Those are spirits that are created when someone gets really upset. They cause all kinds of trouble, like making noises and turning lights on and off and knocking things over."

"Or making a fake tornado go wild?" Ava said.

"Or that," said Gwen.

"What do poltergeists look like?" Aisha asked.

"They don't look like anything," said Gwen. "From what I read, they're usually invisible. Sometimes they might appear as little balls of light, but they don't look like people or anything."

"But you said the thing inside the tornado looked like a girl," Aisha said to Ava.

"It did," Ava confirmed. "And there are the drawings of her. And the photograph."

"Then maybe Rosemary *is* a ghost," said Aisha.

Gwen shook her head. "From what I've read, ghosts can't do much. Like, they can sort of touch you, or maybe make things around them cold or whatever, but they can't make things move or hurt you. They're more like memories or something. Besides, this thing showed up at the house *and* at school. I think ghosts stay in one place."

Ava sighed. "Gwen's right," she said. "Rosemary can

definitely move things. And she's following Cassie. It's almost like Cassie is haunted, not the house. So maybe Rosemary's kind of a combination of these things."

"A polterghost," Aisha said.

"That would be interesting," said Gwen. "And creepy."

"She's definitely creepy," Ava said. "Whatever she is."

"I found one more interesting thing," Gwen said. "A book. It's called *The Summer of the Ghost*. It's about a girl whose house is haunted by the spirit of someone who died there, and how she got it to leave. And it happens to be by Taraji Lang."

"The author of *Sisters in Time*?" Aisha said. "I've never seen that one on the shelf at the library."

"That's because it's not a novel," said Gwen. "It's a true story. It would be in the nonfiction section."

"True?" said Ava. "As in, she had a ghost in her house?"

"Yep," said Gwen. "When she was thirteen. And the school library has a copy. I checked. If we hurry, we can check it out before homeroom."

Now it was finally Ava's turn to tell her friends what she'd learned.

"Lily tried to tell her mother that there was something wrong with Violet," she said. "She wrote her more than a dozen letters. See?"

She took the letters out of her backpack and showed them to Aisha and Gwen.

"But none of them were opened. I don't think they even got mailed. There are stamps on them, but they weren't postmarked. Somehow, Violet got ahold of them. Or maybe Rosemary did. I don't know. But you can tell Lily thought they weren't getting through, because she gets more and more upset when her mother doesn't respond."

The three friends spent the next few minutes looking at the letters. Then the bus arrived at school, and they had to hurry to the library to see if they could check out Taraji Lang's book. Aisha looked it up on the computer and they went to the shelf where it was supposed to be.

"It's not here," Gwen said.

"Maybe Mr. Monday took it out to make a display," Ava suggested. "Since the author is going to be here tomorrow."

They checked out the display, where several of Taraji Lang's books were, but the one they wanted wasn't there. They went to the front desk, where Mr. Monday was checking in books that had been returned.

"Do you know where the copy of *The Summer of the Ghost* by Taraji Lang is?" Ava asked. "It's not on the shelf or in the display."

Mr. Monday typed something on his keyboard. "It's checked out," he said.

"Can you tell us who has it?" Aisha asked. "We kind of need it for a project we're working on. Maybe the person would let us borrow it for a little bit."

Mr. Monday looked at her over his glasses. "That's confidential information," he said.

The girls groaned.

"I'm joking," said Mr. Monday. "The person who checked it out is Beth-Ann Jennings."

All three girls gasped in surprise.

"Is that shocking?" Mr. Monday asked.

"Uh, kind of," said Gwen. "I thought she was more the romance novel type."

Mr. Monday raised an eyebrow. "People can often surprise you," he said. "If you give them a chance."

"Okay," Ava said. "Well, thanks."

The three of them left the library and headed for their homerooms.

"What's she doing with a book like that?" Gwen wondered aloud.

"I don't know," Ava said. "I don't even know how to ask Beth-Ann about it."

"About what?"

The three girls stopped and turned around. Beth-Ann was behind them.

"I heard you say my name," she said.

"No, you didn't," Aisha said.

Beth-Ann rolled her eyes. "Yeah, I did," she said. "Why are you talking about me? I mean besides the fact that I'm way more interesting than the three of you."

"Fine," said Gwen. "We were wondering why you checked out *The Summer of the Ghost*."

"Why do you care?" Beth-Ann snapped.

"We don't," Ava said. "Never mind." She looked at Aisha and Gwen. "It's not important," she said.

The girls started to walk away.

"I know why you're asking," Beth-Ann called out.

Ava turned back. "What?" she said.

"I said, I know why you're asking. About the book."

"Oh yeah?" Gwen said. "Why?"

"Because you think you saw a ghost," said Beth-Ann. "Obviously."

Ava assumed she was teasing them. Beth-Ann had a smug look on her face, as she always did when she was insulting someone. But there was something about the way she'd called out to them that made Ava think there was something else going on. Beth-Ann had wanted them to turn around.

"What do you know about it?" Ava asked.

Beth-Ann walked closer. "Not here," she said. "My house. After school."

Gwen snorted. "You want *us* to come to *your* house?" she said.

"I didn't say I *want* you to," said Beth-Ann. "And if you tell anyone I asked you, I'll say you're lying."

"Like how yesterday you said I was lying about what I saw in the tornado?" Ava said.

"I never said you were lying," Beth-Ann corrected her. "I said I didn't see anything."

"But you did," said Ava. "Didn't you?"

Beth-Ann looked away, but only for a second. She snapped her eyes back to Ava, and they were as sharp as always. "My house," she said. "After school. And if you don't show, I won't help you."

She didn't wait for Ava to respond. She pushed past them and continued on her way down the hall.

"Is she for real?" Aisha said, watching Beth-Ann walk away.

"She just said all that to get attention," said Gwen. "She doesn't know anything about ghosts."

"I think she does," Ava said.

"What?" said Gwen. "You're really going to trust Beth-Ann Jennings?"

"I didn't say I trust her," said Ava as Beth-Ann disappeared around the corner. "But I do think she knows something. And I'm going to find out what it is."

15

Mayor Jennings was not what Ava expected.

"Would you girls like some cookies?" she asked, standing in the doorway of Beth-Ann's bedroom. "I just took them out of the oven. I'm trying something new—lavender chocolate chip. The lavender is from my garden. I'd love to know what you think." She was wearing faded jeans and a T-shirt with the logo of a rock band whose records Ava had heard her parents playing.

"Thanks, Mom," Beth-Ann said, taking the plate from her mother and bringing it back to where the others were sitting on the floor.

"I never thought about the mayor baking cookies," Aisha said as she took a bite.

"Me either," said Ava. "I figured she'd be too busy with meetings and mayor stuff."

Mrs. Jennings laughed. "Oh, I do all that," she said. "But sometimes a mayor has to do fun stuff too. How are the cookies?"

"These are the best thing I've ever tasted," Gwen declared. "Even better than my grandmother's snickerdoodles, although don't tell her I said that."

"She's always trying out new flavors," Beth-Ann told them. "Last week it was coconut and lime cheesecake. It was really good."

"Thanks, girls," the mayor said. "Let me know if you want any more of those."

Ava had waited all day to find out what Beth-Ann had to say about ghosts. Luckily, soccer practice had been canceled after it had started to storm around noon, and there was no play rehearsal scheduled, so all of them had the afternoon free. Now Ava, Aisha, and Gwen were at the Jenningses' house.

The house was also not what Ava had expected. For some reason, she'd thought the mayor would live in a kind of boring house. The Jenningses' house was anything but boring. It was filled with all kinds of colorful paintings, which had been painted by Beth-Ann's artist father. The rooms were stuffed with comfortable furniture that you wouldn't be afraid to curl up on to read a book, and there were cats everywhere. Ava had counted at least nine already, and more seemed to appear every couple of minutes, walking in and out of Beth-Ann's room as if they were making sure everything was okay.

Beth-Ann's room was also a surprise. Given how Beth-Ann acted at school, Ava thought her room would be decorated perfectly and filled with posters of pop singers or actors. Instead, it was messy in a good way, with books everywhere, craft supplies and half-completed projects on the desk and floor, and walls covered in photographs that Beth-Ann had taken herself. They were really good ones, and Ava was now wondering if maybe she'd been wrong about what kind of person Beth-Ann was.

"Okay," Ava said. "We're here. What do you have to tell us?"

"Well, you know about my uncle, right?" Beth-Ann said. "The one who directs TV shows?"

"How could we not?" Gwen teased. "You only talked about being on one of his shows for, like, an entire month."

"Ha-ha," said Beth-Ann. "It was only about a week. Anyway, my uncle's girlfriend is this woman named Chamomile. We call her Cammy. And she's super into ghost hunting. He's tried to get her to let him make a show about her, but she says real ghost hunters don't do it to get famous and all those people you see with TV shows are fakes."

"What exactly does she *do*?" Ava asked.

"Mostly she investigates places that are supposedly

haunted. Usually, they turn out not to be. But sometimes they're the real thing. Cammy is also into UFOs. She was abducted when she was a kid but they returned her a few weeks later. She says sometimes what people think are ghosts are really aliens."

"Cammy sounds interesting," Aisha said.

Beth-Ann nodded. "She is. She took me on a few hunts with her when I was on location with my uncle. Most of them turned out to be nothing. But we did meet one ghost. That's what made me really believe in all of this stuff."

"What kind of ghost was it?" Ava asked her.

"It was a boy," said Beth-Ann. Her voice changed as she talked, and she sounded a little bit sad. "This woman contacted Cammy and said that she'd moved into a new house about six months before, and there was this ghost who kept appearing to her. She was so scared that she wanted to sell the house and move, but everyone who looked at it said they got a terrible feeling being there and nobody would buy it."

"And was it really a ghost?" Gwen asked as she took another cookie from the plate.

"Yeah," said Beth-Ann. "I saw him and everything. He spoke to us. He said his name was Dandy, which we thought was kind of weird, and he kept asking where Malcolm was. Cammy asked the woman if she knew anyone with either of those names, and she said no. But then Cammy got the idea to look up the people who owned the house before the woman bought it, to see if they'd experienced anything weird there."

"And?" Gwen asked.

"At first, they didn't want to talk to her," said Beth-Ann. "But when Cammy told them how scared the woman was, they finally did."

"*And*?" Gwen said again when Beth-Ann grew quiet.

"Malcolm was their little boy," Beth-Ann said. "He'd been very sick and had to spend a lot of time alone in bed. He liked stories, so his parents would tell him ones they made up about a little boy named Danny. But Malcolm had recently lost a tooth, and when he tried to say Danny's name it came out as 'Dandy.' Dandy had all the adventures that Malcolm couldn't."

"So, Dandy wasn't a real person?" said Ava.

Beth-Ann shook her head. "He was made up. But as he got sicker, Malcolm started to talk about Dandy like he was a real person. Like they were friends. He told his parents that Dandy visited him when they weren't around. They thought he was just imagining things because he was sick."

"I don't get it," said Gwen. "If this Dandy kid wasn't real, how could he be a ghost?"

"Cammy thinks that Malcolm *made* him real," Beth-Ann answered. "She thinks he believed in him so much that he brought him to life in a way. Because he wasn't *really* alive. The idea of him was. And that idea took the form of a ghost. Or something like a ghost."

"What's that word you made up this morning, Aisha?" Gwen said.

"A polterghost," Aisha said.

"A polterghost," said Gwen. "Dandy's a polterghost."

Beth-Ann laughed. "Polterghost. I like that. I guess that's kind of what Dandy is. Was. I don't know what words to use. Is a ghost an it?"

"I think we should say *he*," said Gwen. "It's nicer."

"Did Malcolm die?" Ava asked.

"Yeah," said Beth-Ann. "It's a sad story."

"But Dandy stayed around," Ava said, her mind whirling as she worked it all out. "And he was looking for his friend."

"That's what Cammy thinks," Beth-Ann agreed.

"Did she . . . get rid of him?" Aisha asked. "I hate to say it like that, but what else do you call it?"

"Cammy says her job is to help ghosts move on," Beth-Ann said.

"To where?" said Ava.

"Cammy calls it the Next Place," Beth-Ann answered. "I guess people call it different things depending on what they believe."

"And did she do that?" Ava asked. "Get him to go there?"

"And *how* did she do it?" Aisha added.

"There are different ways," Beth-Ann said. "Sometimes you can just ask them. But sometimes they don't want to go, because they're still attached to a place or a person or whatever. Malcolm was the only person Dandy knew, and since Malcolm was dead, he couldn't tell Dandy that it was okay for him to move on too."

"So, he's still in the house?" said Ava.

"As far as I know," said Beth-Ann. "Once Cammy explained to the woman what was happening, she actually felt sorry for Dandy and said he could stay if he wanted to."

Ava sighed. "That's really interesting," she said. "But in my case, I don't want Rosemary staying around. I don't think she's a nice ghost. I think she wants to cause trouble."

"Rosemary," Beth-Ann said. "That's the name you said the other day when the thing with the tornado happened. Do you know who she was?"

"No," Ava said. "We couldn't find any real person with that name. I think she's something—someone—that Violet Blackthorn created somehow when she was dying. And then she stuck around after Violet died, getting angrier and angrier."

"She sounds fun," Beth-Ann said.

Ava laughed. "*So* much fun," she said. "But I'm really worried about what's happening with Cassie. It's like she's turning into Violet Blackthorn or something. Now she even has a fever like Violet did." She looked at Beth-Ann. "Why did you decide to tell us all of this?" she asked.

Beth-Ann smiled. "Because you looked so sad," she said. "The other day at rehearsal. It reminded me of the way Malcolm's parents looked when Cammy and I visited them. And I'm sorry I pretended not to see what happened."

"It's okay," said Ava.

"No, it's not," said Beth-Ann, shaking her head. "I shouldn't have done that."

"Look at you, apologizing," Gwen said. "It's almost like you're not really a mean girl."

"Gwen!" Aisha exclaimed. "That wasn't nice."

"She's right," Beth-Ann said. "I *am* a mean girl. Although I like to think of it more as being truthful. In a sarcastic way."

"Uh-huh," Gwen said.

"What?" said Beth-Ann.

"Sometimes you're funny," said Aisha.

"But sometimes you're just mean," Gwen added.

Beth-Ann shrugged. "I'm still polishing my material," she said. "Anyway, it works for me. I don't care if people like me or not."

"Uh-huh," Gwen said again.

"Would you stop saying that," said Beth-Ann.

"Well, I do," Aisha said. "Like you, I mean."

"Me too," Ava added. "And trust me, everybody is afraid of what other people think about them."

"I haven't decided yet," Gwen said when the others

looked at her. "But I guess I might like you too."

"Whatever," Beth-Ann said, but she was smiling. "Anyway, we still haven't figured out what to do about Rosemary. And from the sound of it, we need to, and soon."

"How about we give Cammy a call?" Gwen suggested. "Maybe she has some ideas."

"She and my uncle are backpacking in Thailand and visiting Cammy's family there," Beth-Ann said. "They won't be back for a month. I don't think we have that much time."

"What about the Taraji Lang book?" said Ava. "That's what got us together in the first place. Is there anything in there that might help?"

"I don't know," Beth-Ann said. "In that book, they have to find the bones of the girl who died and bury them to put her spirit to rest."

"I don't think Rosemary has bones," Ava said. "I mean, I don't think she was a real person."

"I don't think she wants to go, anyway," said Beth-Ann. "I think she's a mean girl too. She gets more out of haunting your sister than she does being nice."

"How about we ask Taraji Lang what she thinks?" Aisha suggested. "She seems to know a lot about ghosts."

"That's a great idea," Ava said. "And she'll be at school tomorrow. But how will we get a chance to talk to her alone? I don't want to ask her about this in front of everyone."

"Leave that to me," Beth-Ann said.

"What are you going to do?" Gwen asked her.

Beth-Ann grinned. "Maybe be a little bit of a mean girl."

16

I wish Cassie was here, Ava thought as she listened to Taraji Lang talk about what it was like to be a writer. *She would love this.*

Once again, though, Cassie wasn't there. She was still home sick. Her fever had gotten worse. Their father had made an appointment with a doctor, but Ava feared that no doctor could help her sister. It was no ordinary fever that Cassie had, she was sure of that, only she couldn't tell their parents because it sounded unbelievable.

"Where do you get your ideas?"

Ava was brought back to attention by the question Bobby Endicott had asked Taraji Lang.

"From anywhere and everywhere," the writer answered. "You never know what's going to inspire you. For instance, my novel *The Girl Who Drank the Sea*. I got the idea for that one when I was lying on a beach in Maui. I looked up and saw this young woman—probably about your age—standing in the water. She was bending down, her face almost touching the surface, like she was looking at her reflection. Then she smiled and laughed, as if the ocean had just told her the best joke. I thought about what that joke might be, and why the girl would be able to understand what the water was saying. And that's how I came up with Nalia, whose mother was a mermaid and whose father was the ghost of a drowned sailor."

Another hand went up. This time Aisha's. Taraji Lang nodded at her. "Yes?"

"What's the best way to become a writer?" Aisha asked.

"Write," said Ms. Lang.

Everybody in the room laughed.

"I'm serious," the author said. "If you want to be a writer, write. Every day, if you can. And don't worry about whether what you're writing is good enough. It probably isn't. Not at first. But if you keep writing, it will get better." She smiled. "I know you were hoping I'd say take this class or study that subject. And yes, you can take classes to learn how to be a better writer. But the most important thing you can do is tell the stories that are inside you. And *all* of you have stories inside you." She pointed her finger at Aisha. "You," she said, then pointed at some others. "And you. And you. And you. Every single one of you. And all of your stories are important. Does that mean you'll all be writers? Of course not. You're all going to be different things. But don't ever forget that your whole life is a story and you are the most important character in it. Okay?"

Aisha, Ava, and all the others nodded.

"All right," said Mr. Monday. "I want to thank Ms. Lang

for coming to talk to us today. And now, as we always do when we have a guest speaker, it's time to draw a name to see who will be joining Ms. Lang for lunch today."

"This is it," Beth-Ann whispered to Ava.

"I've got all of your names on pieces of paper here in this bowl," Mr. Monday said, holding up a red plastic bowl that rattled slightly when he shook it. "I'll pick a name at random, and that person can pick three friends to join them at lunch with—"

"Mr. Monday?" Beth-Ann interrupted.

"Yes?"

"I was just thinking," Beth-Ann said. "Instead of picking a name, how about we have a quiz to see who gets to have lunch with Ms. Lang?"

"A quiz?" Mr. Monday said.

Beth-Ann nodded. "Right," she said. "I mean, some of us are really big fans of her books. Other people have never even read her. I think someone who has questions about the books should get to go, not just someone who gets picked out of a bowl and might not really *want* to go."

"We always do it this way, Beth-Ann," Mr. Monday said, and started to reach into the bowl.

"I know," said Beth-Ann. "But."

Mr. Monday stopped. Beth-Ann was using her mean-girl voice, the one that Ava had heard her use before when she wanted to get her way about something. It had always irritated her. Now that she knew there was more to Beth-Ann than most people saw, she had to keep herself from laughing.

"But what, Beth-Ann?" Mr. Monday said.

"Well, it's just that my mother—the *mayor*—always says that the reward should go to the person who worked the hardest for it. Doesn't that seem more fair?"

Ava couldn't imagine Mrs. Jennings saying any such thing, and she suspected Beth-Ann had made that up. Mr. Monday, though, sighed and set the bowl down.

"Okay," he said. "How about this. Ms. Lang can ask trivia questions about her books. The first person to answer three of them correctly gets to have lunch with her."

"And bring three friends," Beth-Ann reminded him. "One for each correct answer."

"And bring three friends," Mr. Monday agreed. "Is that all right with you?" he asked the writer.

"Sounds good to me," said Ms. Lang. "Let's find out which one of you is a Taraji Lang superfan."

Fifteen minutes later, Beth-Ann, Ava, Gwen, and Aisha were sitting at a table in the cafeteria with the author.

"I can't believe you got the first three questions right," Ms. Lang said. "I tried to come up with really hard ones to make it more interesting."

"I'm a big fan," Beth-Ann said. "Do you mind if I—we— ask you some questions?"

"Not at all," said Ms. Lang. "What do you want to know?"

"How do you get a polterghost to leave?" Gwen blurted out.

"Polterwhat?" said Ms. Lang.

"Polterghost," Aisha repeated. "It's kind of a ghost and kind of a poltergeist."

"I've never heard of such a thing," Ms. Lang said.

"We made it up," Ava said quickly. "For a story we're working on."

"Right," Beth-Ann said. "A story. Like you said, if we want to be writers, we should always be writing. So, how would you get it to leave?"

"I'm not sure I know," the author answered. "I know with poltergeists, they usually leave when the person who caused them to manifest realizes what they've done and tells them to leave."

"We can't do that," Gwen said. "She's dead."

"In the story," Aisha added.

"Yeah, in the story," said Gwen.

"And it's not really a ghost," Ava added. "Because it's not the spirit of someone who died. Let's say the person who *is* dead kind of created her by accident, but it all went wrong."

"Hmm," Ms. Lang said. "I don't think I entirely

understand, but I'm sure you'll work out the details as you write your story. What I *think* you're saying is that someone caused this—"

"Polterghost," Gwen said.

"This polterghost to manifest. Then she died before she could do anything about it and it's still around causing trouble. Is that it?"

"Exactly," Ava said.

"That really is a good story," Ms. Lang said.

"We think so," said Beth-Ann. "So, how would you go about getting rid of the polterghost if you were writing the story?"

"I'm not sure I should tell you," Ms. Lang said.

"What?" said Gwen. "Why not?"

Ms. Lang laughed. "Because it's your story," she said. "It sounds to me like you're stuck and want someone to help you out."

"That's *exactly* what's happening," Ava said.

Ms. Lang nodded. "I understand," she said. "As writers,

sometimes we don't know where to take our stories."

"So how do you figure it out?" Aisha asked.

"Well, speaking for myself, sometimes I just pick a direction and see what happens."

"Not helpful," Gwen muttered.

"Okay," Ms. Lang said. "I'll give you *one* suggestion. If this polterghost was created by someone who died, maybe you could bring *her* back."

"What do you mean?" Beth-Ann asked.

"Summon the ghost of the dead person," Ms. Lang said. "Maybe she can deal with the polterghost."

"That's brilliant," said Gwen.

"But how do we bring her back?" said Aisha.

"That problem I'm leaving up to *you* to figure out," Ms. Lang said. "And when you finish this story, I want to be the first one to read it."

They spent the rest of lunch talking about Taraji Lang's books. When they were done, she surprised them by giving them each a signed copy of *Sisters in Time*.

"Could you sign mine to my sister instead?" Ava asked her when it was her turn to get a book. "She really loves your books, but she couldn't be here today because she's sick."

"What's her name?" Ms. Lang asked.

"Cassie," Ava said.

"They're twins," Gwen announced.

"Really?" Ms. Lang said. "I'm a twin too. And I know my sister Sanaa and I never liked to share books. How about I sign one for each of you?"

"Thank you," Ava said. "I really appreciate that."

"Here you go," Ms. Lang said, handing Ava two books. "I have to tell you, I do a lot of school visits, but this has been one of the most fun. And I mean it—I want to read this story of yours. I can't wait to see how it ends."

"Us too," Gwen said.

When she got home from school, Ava found her mother in the kitchen.

"How did it go at the doctor?" Ava asked her.

"It was the strangest thing," her mother said. "As soon as we got there, Cassie's fever completely disappeared. The doctor couldn't find anything wrong with her at all."

"Where is she now?"

"Upstairs," her mother said.

"I'm glad she's better," Ava said. "Hey, would it be okay if I had some girls over for another sleepover tomorrow night?"

"Gwen and Aisha?"

"Plus a new friend," Ava said. "Her name is Beth-Ann. Her mom is the mayor."

"The mayor, huh?" said her mother. "You're making friends with all the important people in town, I see. Sure, they can come over. I think Cassie is fine, although the doctor suggested keeping her home one more day, just in case."

"Great," Ava said. "And thanks."

She went upstairs and headed right to Cassie's room. As

it always seemed to be lately, the door was shut. Ava knocked on it.

"Who is it?" Cassie called out. She sounded annoyed.

"Me," Ava said. "I have a surprise for you."

A moment later, the door opened. Cassie stood in the doorway. Her face was flushed, and her eyes looked weirdly shiny. "What is it?"

Ava took the book Taraji Lang had signed out of her backpack. "This," she said.

Cassie took the book. "Thanks," she said, and started to shut the door.

"Aren't you even going to look inside?" Ava asked.

"Later," Cassie said shortly. "I'm busy."

"Doing what?" Ava said. She was annoyed by how rude Cassie was being.

"Homework," Cassie said, and shut the door in Ava's face.

Ava turned and walked to her room. She was angry at her sister's behavior. Even more, though, she was worried about her. Something bad was happening to Cassie. Her fever might have disappeared when she was at the doctor, but given how she looked, Ava was pretty sure it had come back.

"Hang on until tomorrow, Cassie," she whispered. "We have a plan."

She, Gwen, Aisha, and Beth-Ann had thought of something.

She hoped it would work.

17

"We'll be back in a couple of hours," Ava's father said as he got into the car. "Ed helped us find an antique store that has the light fixtures we need for the living room, so we're going to go pick them up. You can order pizza or whatever you want for dinner."

"Okay," Ava said, waving.

"This is perfect," Beth-Ann said as the car pulled out of the driveway. "I was wondering how we would get this done with them around."

The four girls turned and looked at Blackthorn House.

"The roses are even thicker now," Ava said. "And look,

they're halfway up the walls of the summerhouse. It's like they're trying to eat it."

Beth-Ann looked at the summerhouse. "I think that's where we should try to summon Violet's ghost," she said. "Something tells me it's the heart of this place."

"I think you might be right," Ava said. "She and Lily did spend a lot of time in there that summer."

"We're being watched," Aisha said.

"By who?" asked Ava.

"Cassie," Aisha answered. "She's looking out her window."

Ava looked up. Sure enough, her sister's face was framed in the bedroom window. Cassie scowled, then turned away.

"Let's get started," Beth-Ann said.

The friends went into the summerhouse. With the roses growing over a lot of the windows, it was hot, dark, and stuffy inside. There was just enough light getting through that they could see.

"Did you find what I asked for?" Beth-Ann said to Ava. "Something that belonged to Violet?"

"I think so," Ava said. "This was in the box of stuff I got from Ed." She reached into her pocket and took out a delicate silver chain that had a silver locket dangling from it. The locket was shaped like a rose. On the back were the initials *VB*.

"Violet Blackthorn," Beth-Ann said. "It's got to be. Is there anything inside?"

Ava opened the locket and showed it to Beth-Ann and the others. Inside, someone had scratched the same figure of the screaming girl that was on Cassie's bedroom wall.

"It's Rosemary," she said.

"That's creepy," Gwen said. "She should have a picture of her sister in there."

"She probably did," said Aisha. "Then it got replaced with this."

"It will have to do," said Beth-Ann, taking it from Ava. "Okay, let's sit in a circle on the floor."

"What are we doing, exactly?" Aisha asked as they took their places.

"We're going to ask Violet to help us," Beth-Ann said.

"That's it?" said Gwen, sounding disappointed. "Shouldn't we have candles? And a spell or something?"

"We're not witches," Beth-Ann said. "And this isn't magic."

"Then how do you know it will work?" said Gwen. "Why should a ghost care about what we want?"

"All we can do is try," Ava said. "Cassie needs our help. She needs Violet's help."

"I'm just saying, it looks way more complicated in the movies," said Gwen.

Beth-Ann set the locket on the floor in the center of the circle. "Okay," she said. "Here goes. Violet Blackthorn, we'd, um, like to speak with you. Please."

"What?" said Gwen. "No ghost is going to answer to that."

"You think you can do better?" said Beth-Ann.

"Yeah, I do," said Gwen. "First, we need to, like, set the mood. Everybody take a deep breath."

"This is ridiculous," Beth-Ann said. "Cammy never—"

"Cammy isn't here, is she?" Gwen said. "Deep breath."

Beth-Ann breathed in dramatically, then let it out.

"Good," Gwen said. "Again." All four of them breathed deeply. "Now, imagine the circle here is filled with golden light. It's a safe place to be. Nothing bad can happen here."

Ava did as Gwen suggested. She saw them all sitting in a warm, happy place.

Gwen cleared her throat. "We call on the spirit of Violet Blackthorn," she said in a solemn voice. "We call you with this locket. Join us in our circle and give us a sign that you hear me."

"Oh, that's *so* much better," Beth-Ann said. "I'm sure she'll—"

"Uh, you guys," Ava said.

"Ghosts don't care about fancy language," Beth-Ann said, ignoring her.

"It's called being polite," said Gwen.

"You guys!" Ava said, silencing their argument.

In the center of their circle, right above the locket, the air was shimmering. Small electric-blue sparks danced in the air.

"What is that?" Aisha said.

"Ectoplasm," said Beth-Ann. "It's like ghost glitter."

The sparks multiplied, forming a shape. A moment later, the figure of a girl appeared.

"Told you," Gwen said to Beth-Ann.

"That's Violet," Ava said. "She looks just like her photographs."

The ghost of Violet Blackthorn faded in and out as she looked around the summerhouse. She looked exactly as she did in the pictures of her, wearing an old-fashioned white dress. Her dark hair hung in two braids down her back.

"Why am I here?" she asked in a faint voice.

"We called you," Ava said. "We need you to help us."

Violet looked at her. "Help you?" she said. "How?"

"You need to tell your girl Rosemary to go away," Gwen said.

At the mention of Rosemary's name, Violet flickered.

"No!" Ava shouted. "Don't go! Rosemary is trying to hurt my sister!"

Violet reappeared, but she was barely visible. She didn't speak.

"Rosemary is trying to do to my sister—Cassie—what she did to you," Ava explained. "We don't know how to get rid of her. Can you help us?"

The ghost shook its head.

"Please," Ava said. "There has to be a way."

Violet opened her mouth. At the same time, a loud rumble of thunder rolled overhead. Then the sound of rain pounded on the roof. What little light filled the summerhouse disappeared, and the girls were left in darkness. All that was visible was the faint blue apparition of Violet Blackthorn.

"She's here," the ghost whispered, and vanished.

The door to the summerhouse blew open. Wind and rain came roaring in, and the girls were pelted with cold, hard drops. In the open doorway a cloud of darkness swirled. Then it took the form of a girl—a girl with black holes for eyes and wild hair that stuck out all around. The figure looked less like a real person and more like the drawing on Cassie's wall. Only now it was the size of a real person.

"Rosemary," Ava whispered.

A dark hole appeared in the spirit's face, a mouth that opened and kept opening. Then a scream poured out. The sound was terrible. It filled the summerhouse with a piercing shriek so loud that all four girls clapped their hands over their ears to try to block it. But that didn't work. The sound coming from Rosemary was inescapable.

The wind and rain began to swirl, stinging the girls' eyes and making it difficult to see anything at all. They stood up and felt for one another. Ava reached out and touched a hand. She slipped her fingers between those of whomever it belonged to and held tight.

"Make a circle!" she shouted.

Rosemary wailed and took a step farther into the summerhouse.

"Take my hand!" Aisha shouted.

"Got it!" said Gwen. "Beth-Ann?"

"I'm here," Beth-Ann called.

A second later, Ava felt someone take her other hand. "Is everyone holding two hands?" she called.

"Yes," the others answered at the same time.

Ava wasn't sure what to do now. All she knew was that she had to do *something*. She looked toward the door and saw that Rosemary was growing. Her head was now almost to the ceiling. The screaming coming from her gaping mouth was unbearable. Ava feared that in just a few moments, they would all be consumed by the storm of rage and darkness coming from the spirit.

"Violet!" Ava cried out. "Violet, please. Help us."

There was no answer. No sparkle of blue light. Nothing.

"She's too frightened," Beth-Ann said. "She can't face Rosemary."

"Please!" Ava shouted. "Someone! Anyone!"

A moment later, the air in front of Ava began to glow. But it wasn't with blue light. This light was silver. And the figure it formed wasn't that of a girl. It was of an old woman.

"Lily?" Ava said.

The ghost smiled. Then she turned to face Rosemary. "Get out!" she ordered. "Get out, and leave them be!"

The shadowy thing that was Rosemary shrieked as it shrank back to the size of a girl. The darkness rushed out the door of the summerhouse like water retreating into a drain. Ava now saw that Aisha was on her left and Beth-Ann was on her right. The ghost of Lily Blackthorn was still standing, in the center of the circle.

"Is she gone?" Ava asked.

Lily shook her head. "No," she said. "She's gone into the big house."

"Cassie is in there!" Ava said. "We have to help her."

She let go of the hands she was holding and ran for the door. As she did, the ghost of Lily Blackthorn winked out. But Ava wasn't thinking about Lily. She was thinking about Cassie. She pounded up the porch steps and hit the door. It opened with a bang as she ran into the house.

"Cassie!" she shouted. "Cassie! Are you okay?"

There was no answer, so Ava ran up the stairs as her friends came into the house.

"Ava!" Beth-Ann shouted. "Be careful!"

Ava reached the second floor and ran to Cassie's room. This time, the door was open. Ava stepped inside.

Cassie's room was filled with the same swirling blackness that had been in the summerhouse. Cassie stood in the center of it. Her arms were at her sides, and she was staring at something. It was the full-length mirror that hung on one of her walls. Ava looked at it, and inside she saw Rosemary. Her clawlike hand was sticking out into the room.

Ava watched as Cassie lifted her own hand and stepped forward.

"Cassie! No!" Ava yelled. "Don't go with her!"

Cassie turned her head and looked at her sister.

"Come." Rosemary's voice seeped out of the mirror, cold and dark as rainwater. "Forever."

Cassie looked away from her sister. She took another step. Her fingertips touched the darkness of Rosemary's spirit figure.

"Cassie!" Ava cried.

She lurched forward, reaching for her sister. At the same time, Rosemary wrapped her fingers around Cassie's wrist and pulled Cassie toward her and into the mirror. Cassie's body was surrounded by blackness. Then it seemed to dissolve as Cassie was sucked through the mirror. Rosemary laughed as the glass shattered into thousands of tiny pieces and fell onto the floor.

Ava screamed in frustration as her friends came into the room. They looked at the broken glass on the floor.

"What happened?" Beth-Ann asked.

"Rosemary took her," said Ava. "She's gone."

"Gone where?" Gwen said.

"I don't know!" Ava said. "Wherever spirits take people."

She began to cry. Tears ran down her cheeks, and she sat down on Cassie's bed. "I couldn't help her," she sobbed.

Aisha sat down beside her and put her arm around Ava's shoulders. Ava wanted her to say that everything would be all right. When she didn't, Ava felt her last bit of hope disappear.

"She won," she said. "Rosemary won. She got Cassie just like she got Violet."

"No," a voice said.

Ava looked up. The ghost of Lily Blackthorn stood near the mirror, looking at the broken glass. "Your sister is still in this house," Lily said. "Rosemary can't take her. She has to die for that to happen."

"Where is she?" Ava asked.

Lily shook her head. "That, I do not know," she said. "Somewhere Rosemary feels she can keep her hidden."

Ava thought. "I know," she said.

"Where?" said Beth-Ann.

Ava pointed toward the attic. "The angels' nest."

18

The moment they stepped into the attic, Ava knew that she was right.

The space was filled with a darkness that was different from ordinary dark. It was thicker somehow, like fog. She could feel it swirling around her, touching her skin, as if it was trying to swallow her up. She shivered. She wanted to leave immediately, to go back to the light she could see in the stairway behind her. But Cassie was in there—she was sure of it—and she had to rescue her before the darkness took her away forever.

Fortunately, Aisha had brought a small flashlight with

her. She turned it on, and a thin beam of light pierced the darkness. It didn't go very far, though, as if the blackness was too thick for it to get through.

"There's no one here," Gwen said.

"They're up there," said Ava, pointing to the opening in the ceiling. Aisha aimed the flashlight at it, and they could see the darkness coming down out of it, like the tentacles of an octopus searching for prey.

Beside Ava, there was a glimmer of light, and once again the ghost of Lily Blackthorn materialized. Ava momentarily thought how strange it was that seeing and talking to a ghost now felt totally normal. She wasn't afraid of Lily at all.

"The angels' nest," Lily said, sounding both happy and sad. "Violet and I used to hide up there to read or listen to the rain on the roof. It was our secret place. Once Rosemary came, it became their place, and I never went up there again."

"It's like Rosemary replaced you as her sister," Beth-Ann said.

"Yes," said Lily. "It wasn't Violet's fault. She didn't know what was happening, because of the fever. It was the fever that brought Rosemary to her. Rosemary fed on it."

"A fever ghost," Gwen said. "That's even worse than a polterghost."

"The fever caused Violet to have delusions," Lily explained. "She thought Rosemary was a friend. A sister. And the more Rosemary took from her, the stronger she became, until there was nothing left of Violet."

"But Violet's ghost didn't stay here when she died," Aisha asked. "Why?"

"We spirits exist in our own realm," said Lily. "Sometimes we travel back and forth. Sometimes we do get stuck in one place or another. Rosemary is not a ghost. She's something different. She can only exist here."

"So then where is she trying to take Cassie?" Ava asked, not sure if she wanted to know the answer.

Lily hesitated a moment. "I think she believes she can make your sister like she is. Only she can't. All she can do is . . ." Her voice trailed off, as if saying the last words was too difficult.

Ava understood what she meant, though.

"She'll kill her," she said.

Lily's ghost nodded. "And Rosemary will still exist, angrier than she was before."

"Then what can we do?" Beth-Ann said.

"My sister made Rosemary," Lily said. "I believe she's the only one who can unmake her. But she's afraid of her. I need to convince her to help us."

"You work on that, then," said Ava. "In the meantime, I'm getting Cassie out of that room. Someone help me get the dresser under that opening."

Beth-Ann and Gwen went with her to where the dresser had been moved away from the entrance to the angels' nest. As they moved it across the floor, the darkness pushed back against them. The dresser slid back a foot.

"Oh no you don't," Gwen said, grunting. "I'm not letting some fever ghost beat me. Everybody, push!"

The girls pushed. The dresser moved forward again. When it was under the opening, Ava climbed on top. She stared up into the blackness.

"Cassie?" she called.

There was no answer.

Ava jumped up and grabbed hold of the edge of the opening. A great force slammed down on her, and she fell back down.

"I need your help," she said to Beth-Ann and Gwen. "I can't do this alone."

The other two girls climbed up on the dresser and knelt down. Aisha held the flashlight. They joined their hands together to form a kind of step. Ava put her foot on it and rested her hands on Gwen's and Beth-Ann's heads.

"One," Gwen said. "Two. Three."

On three, the girls stood, lifting Ava with them. She felt pressure as her head pushed through the darkness. It was like diving into water. She couldn't see anything, but her hands touched the floor of the angels' nest. She threw herself onto it. The darkness was suffocating. Ava had to force herself to breathe. All around her there was a crushing weight and a feeling of sadness and anger.

"Cassie?" she said.

There was no answer, so Ava began feeling around with her hands. After just a moment, she touched something. It was a foot. She moved closer, running her hand up Cassie's body until she was next to her sister.

"Cassie?" she said again, shaking her gently.

"Ava?" Cassie's voice was faint.

"I'm here, Cassie," Ava said. "Can you wake up?"

Cassie stirred a little, trying to sit up.

"No," a voice hissed.

Ava felt something move in the darkness around them.

"She's not your sister, Rosemary," Ava said. "Let her go."

A low whine began, like a child crying. It grew louder. Ava, remembering the horrible shrieking that had filled the summerhouse, knew it was going to get worse.

"Cassie," Ava said. "We have to go. Please wake up."

She felt something pulling at her. Long, thin fingers wrapped around her ankle. She immediately pictured the stick figure of Rosemary and imagined it stepping off the wall and coming to life.

"My sister," Rosemary said. "Mine."

"No," Ava said, kicking out. But the darkness clung to her like honey.

"I've been waiting for her," said Rosemary. Her voice slipped around Ava, filling her head. "Waiting so long."

Ava, who was cradling Cassie in her arms, felt her sister soften, as if she was disappearing. She felt Rosemary pull at Cassie.

"Help!" Ava cried out. "Lily! Violet! Someone! She's taking Cassie!"

As the darkness enveloped her, Ava saw a twinkle of blue break through it. Then more sparkles appeared, like tiny fireflies in the night. The dots of light swirled around one another until they settled into the form of Violet Blackthorn. She looked at Ava, and Ava could see that she was afraid too.

"You can do it," Ava encouraged her. "Please."

Violet nodded. "Rosemary," she said. "I'm here. Leave Cassie alone. She belongs with her sister."

"Violet," Rosemary whispered. "You left me alone."

"You don't belong in this place," Violet said. "You belong with me."

As Ava watched, Violet opened her arms.

"Come here," Violet said.

At first, Ava thought the ghost was speaking to her. But then she felt Rosemary's grip on her loosen. She saw something move, coming into the light formed by Violet's aura. It was Rosemary. She looked like the terrifying drawing now, all scratches and hard lines. Ava saw Violet dim, as if she was going to disappear again.

Then Violet's light grew stronger.

"Come here," Violet said. "My sister."

Rosemary moved into the circle created by Violet's arms. As she did, she changed from the horrifying shape of the drawing into the form of a girl.

"My sister," she said as Violet hugged her close. She laid her head on Violet's shoulder.

Violet's blue light surrounded Rosemary. It filled her up, growing brighter and brighter. Violet hugged Rosemary to her, and Rosemary was slowly pulled into Violet's body, until she disappeared completely.

Violet looked over at Ava. "She's part of me again," she said.

"Thank you," Ava said.

Violet nodded. Then she began to fade. As she did, the blue light turned to white, and the angels' nest returned to normal. The last lingering traces of daylight crept in through the windows. When Ava looked at the walls, there were no drawings of Rosemary, only the faded roses on the old wallpaper.

"What happened? How did we get up here?"

Cassie looked up at Ava, confusion on her face. "And why are you holding me like I'm a doll or something?"

Ava hugged her sister and laughed. "It's a long story," she

said. "But trust me, you're going to love it. Now, let's get out of here."

She got down first, then helped Cassie lower herself from the opening in the ceiling.

"Welcome back," Beth-Ann said.

"Uh, hi," said Cassie. She looked at Ava, obviously confused as to why the meanest girl in school was standing in their attic.

"Like I said, it's a long story," said Ava.

"But it has a happy ending," Aisha said.

"What happened down here?" Ava asked them. "How did Lily get Violet to help us?"

"Lily?" Cassie said. "Violet? As in the Blackthorn twins?"

"Yep," said Gwen. "I *told* you your house was haunted."

"Lily reminded Violet that the love sisters have for each other is always stronger than anything that's trying to pull them apart," Beth-Ann said.

"Well, she's right about that," Ava said. She put her arms around Cassie and hugged her tightly. "I love you so much."

"I love you too," Cassie said. "And I really can't wait to find out what's been going on."

"Come on," Gwen said, heading for the stairs. "We'll tell you all about it. But first, we're ordering pizza. I'm starving."

THREE MONTHS LATER

Ava stepped out of her room and into the hallway. Cassie was standing outside her own room, looking toward the stairs.

"Did you hear something?" Ava asked.

Cassie nodded. The sisters walked toward each other, meeting at the top of the stairs.

"Maybe some of the guests are still here," Cassie said.

"It's three o'clock in the morning," Ava reminded her. "The party ended hours ago."

"Well, *someone* is down there," Cassie said. "I can see the lights from the Christmas tree."

The first annual Blackthorn House holiday party had been a lot of fun. With the house finally restored, Ava and Cassie's parents had thrown a huge celebration, inviting everyone in the neighborhood. At least half the residents of Ebenezer had come, filling the house with laughter and holiday cheer. Gwen, Aisha, Beth-Ann, Ava, and Cassie had exchanged presents, and so many cookies had been eaten that Ava was pretty sure she would never eat sugar again. At least for a few days, anyway.

Now, though, something had awakened the twins from their sleep.

"Let's check it out," Ava said, starting down the stairs.

"Really?" Cassie said. "What if it's a burglar?"

"In this town?" Ava said. "It's more likely to be Santa showing up a few nights early. Come on."

Cassie joined her, and together they crept down the stairs. They walked to the living room and looked through the doorway, where they paused and looked at the two figures standing in the room. Violet and Lily Blackthorn had their backs to the sisters. Through them Ava and Cassie could see the Christmas tree, a twelve-foot fir decorated with thousands of lights and hundreds of ornaments. It blazed with soft, warm light.

"They're back," Ava said.

The ghosts turned around. When they saw Ava and Cassie, they smiled.

"Just for one last visit," Lily said. "We wanted to see the house now that your family has made it like it was again."

"It's beautiful," Violet said. "Thank you."

Ava asked the question that had jumped into her mind like a snowstorm. "And Rosemary?" she said.

"Gone," Violet said.

"Forever," said Lily.

"Will we see you again?" Cassie asked.

"Perhaps," said Lily. "One day. But this is your house now. Yours to fill with laughter and happiness and memories."

"With friends," said Violet. She took Lily's hand.

"It's time for us to go," said Lily. "Merry Christmas."

"Merry Christmas," Ava and Cassie said as the two ghosts faded out.

"You know, it used to be a tradition to tell ghost stories around the fire at Christmas," Cassie told Ava.

"Oh yeah?" said Ava. "Well, if anyone decides to revive that tradition, we've got a really good one to tell."

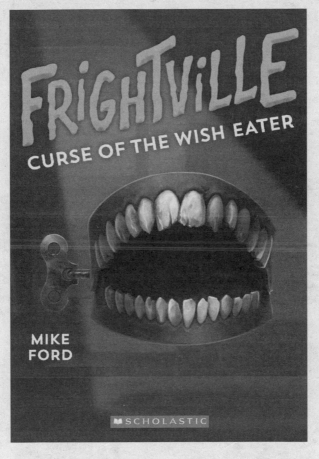

Don't be scared . . . make a wish.

HOME BASE

YOUR FAVORITE BOOKS COME TO LIFE IN A BRAND-NEW DIGITAL WORLD!

- Meet your favorite characters
- Play games
- Create your own avatar
- Chat and connect with other fans
- Make your own comics
- Discover new worlds and stories
- And more!

Start your adventure today! Download the **HOME BASE** app and scan this image to unlock exclusive rewards!

SCHOLASTIC.COM/HOMEBASE

ABOUT THE AUTHOR

Mike Ford is the author of numerous spooky books, including titles in the Eerie, Indiana, Spinetinglers, and Frightville series. He started writing about haunted things after growing up in a house full of ghosts who wanted him to tell them bedtime stories.